NUMBER FOUR

Books by
MOLLY CONE

NUMBER FOUR

● ● ● ●

BY MOLLY CONE

Houghton Mifflin Company Boston 1972

Remembering
Jonny Kyle Richards

CONTENTS

NUMBER FOUR

1

Geraldine

GERALDINE was not the first to know about the accident. But she was definitely the only one to perceive that something important had started to happen to Benjamin. She felt it. Like drums in the back of her head.

Geraldine Slater was fifteen years old and knew some things before they happened. Though no one would suspect it by her moonfull face. Certainly there was nothing especially sensitive about the rest of her family.

Her mother was full moon, all over. Her father looked like one of his own logging trucks which rumbled through the main street every few minutes all the day long. Particularly when he wore his hunting hat, which he hardly took off during the hunting season, not even to sit down to eat breakfast. A red top on a square cab, solidly constructed.

Her brother Harold was something else again. Geraldine really didn't understand Harold. Which was all right with Harold. At seventeen he had not even begun to try to understand himself.

He was no good at football, too wobbly-kneed for basketball, too lazy for track, and politely disrespectful to anybody in town over thirty, including the high school principal. He had no views about sending space ships to the moon, lowering the draft, cheating in exams, getting out of Vietnam, or getting into college.

Benjamin Turner was his best friend.

Benjamin and Harold were close. Not as close though as Benjamin was to his brother, David.

David Turner was quite a bit older than Benjamin. Good-looking too. Girls looked at him almost the same way they always looked at Benjamin. The way they never looked at Harold.

The town of Douglas was tight-lipped about a lot of things that December, 1969. And the way the girls looked at Benjamin was one of them.

Douglas was three blocks long with a motel at one end and a trailer camp at the other. Three gas stations, two restaurants, one supermarket. The library was in a little old house built by an early settler. He named the town. The doctor's office shared a storefront with an insurance agent. The bank was on a corner in a building of its own.

Business flowed as steadily as the trucks through the

main street. The trucks were loaded with logs. Big ones. The monsters of the forest. Western red cedar, Sitka spruce, Douglas fir or western hemlock. Rolling in to the mills and back empty to the logging areas.

Douglas was the center of things measuring by loggers, hunters or fishermen. But, generally speaking, it was close to nothing at all. It was the nadir if you were used to tall buildings, paved sidewalks, lampposts on every corner, delicatessens, transit systems, apartment buildings, and department stores. It was just a little town. Not on the way to any place. It wasn't on the way from any place either. Except the village of Salt Chuck.

In the Slater kitchen, the radio crackled. Harold fiddled with it some more. The voice finally emerged like a duck out of the drizzle. The Slaters listened without much interest at first. The dry staccato of the radio voice splattered like rain on their shingle roof.

"Harsh winter winds roared up the Pacific Coast last night, ripping out power lines, downing trees and endangering boats—and left at least one driver stranded in his car in the near freezing temperatures."

Geraldine shivered. She heard the wind again. Last night it was a giant thing. Wild. Flapping against the windows of her bedroom. Slamming against the roof of the house. Whanging on the garage door. The sound ripped around the outside of the house. It sounded like the screeching of a million sea gulls. It sounded as if the wind were tearing the night into shreds.

". . . This morning David Turner was found dead in his car at rest in a ditch nine miles west of Douglas at Salt Chuck Road. Damage to Turner's car was estimated at fifty dollars."

Clumsily, Harold turned it off. "Wow!" he said. That's all he said. "Wow."

Geraldine stared at the syrup oozing around her waffle.

"Too bad," said her father. Not particularly regretfully. He went on eating his breakfast.

"Poor devil," her mother said.

When one of her father's truck drivers was killed, it was "poor soul," Geraldine remembered. She couldn't help noticing that it was "poor devil" for David Turner. It was plain to Geraldine exactly what the distinction was. She had lived in Douglas most of her life.

"That's Benjamin Turner's brother," Geraldine said. It was a dumb thing to say, she knew as soon as she said it. Everyone living in Douglas knew everyone else. By the time the weekly newspaper came out, there wasn't much printed that everyone hadn't already talked about.

Her mother looked at her father. When Geraldine was a little girl they spelled things out over her head. Like hide the c-a-n-d-y. Now they sent complicated signals. It would have been better, she thought, if they had stuck to spelling. She had never improved much in that category. The signals she was expert at intercepting. Two rapid winks from her mother to her father meant, Don't get excited. A retracting of nostrils from her father to her mother accented by the appearance of two small lines like an equal sign across the bridge of his nose meant, You keep still and let me handle this.

The real danger signal was when her father's neck grew red. He had a short neck and the red had no room to spread out. It concentrated. Bright like his hat. The danger signal for her mother was when her eyes glistened in a popped-out sort of way. But this was Sunday morning. It was a day of rest. And she guessed that neither felt like starting an argument.

The cold mist clung breathily to the windows. Inside, the electric coffee pot hiccupped and began to gurgle. Referee of some kind of a game. Her father tossed back the ball with an unfussed underhand — "Well, Benjamin Turner is smart — for an Indian."

Her mother hurried in to catch it, any old way, before it landed foul. "Well, no one expects those Indian kids to be smart." Her voice was soft as a mitt, padded with generous understanding. "The way they live — and all."

Salt Chuck was the Indian reservation. Just a small village. Geraldine saw it through her mother's eyes. Down sixteen miles of narrow dirt road. Through logging slash and skimpy green forest. Then round the hill and the first sight of the ocean. A gasp of hurtling waves, blue-gray sky, and a stretch of ocean beach. The next rise tore the vista from your sight and you were in the village. Like a bang on the head. The settlement lay, scrubbily, across the road from the driftwood-piled beach. It strung along the river. Some of the houses were falling down. Others looked as if they were soon going to. You hardly noticed the neat ones. The unplanted yards held odds and ends of discarded things. Like wrecked cars and burned-out washing machines. A big yellow bus brought the children from the reservation to Douglas to school each morning. And carried them quickly back again when school was over.

Geraldine couldn't quite think of Benjamin Turner as an Indian. Maybe because he didn't live on the reservation. He lived in Douglas, in a trailer.

Harold said something. Practical Harold. Down-to-earth Harold. There was no sentiment in Harold. As usual, he was about as subtle as two left feet. He said — "I guess maybe Benjamin's father will be giving him the car."

2

The Principal

THE PRINCIPAL of the high school passed a car being pulled out of the ditch earlier that morning. But he didn't know whose it was. Not until hours later. And then the burden of his own morning somewhat crowded out his thoughts about Benjamin Turner.

The principal and his father-in-law spent three hours hunting. A light drift of snow made tracking deer easy. Too easy.

Later, he followed his father-in-law back to the camper, letting him put a pot of coffee on the stove while he stood outside blowing on his hands and hearing details of the accident.

Hunters dotted the forest meadow like ducks on a pond. Campers parked, huddled together at the end of the narrow logging road. No one had even come close to knocking down a deer. Except the principal.

"That was a bad accident," he said when he joined his father-in-law in the camper. He sat down at the tray-sized table and poured a mug full of the steaming coffee.

For a second the older man waited, with his spoonful of sugar suspended in the air. A small craft holding. A hummingbird hovering. Frozen for a second in still life.

"An Indian," Principal Haley said.

"Oh, an Indian," he said, like you say lamppost, or tree or dog, and let the sugar fall into his cup. He tasted the coffee, added sugar, and swallowed two mouthfuls. "Drunk, I suppose."

"They didn't say."

"Indians can't drink," he pronounced, as if he were an expert on the subject. He had lived side by side with Indians all his life, he was fond of saying, and never had any trouble with them. *They don't bother us and we don't bother them* was the way he put it. A *modus vivendi*, the principal thought. Which was a kind of temporary arrangement that had become a way of living. Like poured cement hardening into a solid form.

"Kept the motor running. To keep warm, I guess. When they found him he was dead. Carbon monoxide poisoning."

"A defective muffler," his father-in-law diagnosed. "Most of those Indians don't know how to maintain a car. Take a good look next time you get down to their village. When their cars don't run anymore, they just leave them sitting in their front yards."

The principal reached over to the child-sized stove and picked up the loud bubbling pot. He refilled his coffee mug. He didn't mind it strong. A change from the instant in the teachers' lounge at school.

As principal of the Douglas High School, Gregory E. Haley made a point of showing an interest in things. Drinking tea-bag tea at the PTA meetings. Sitting half-frozen through all the high school football games. Going hunting.

Truthfully, he didn't much care for hunting. He admitted it to himself. And to almost no one else. His secret worry was that he had never felt completely at home in Douglas. Because of that, perhaps, he walked with his shoulders held stiffly erect, and his head well up. He spoke, on occasion, a little louder and more firmly than he might have, had he fitted in easily. He was naturally rather standoffish with his staff of teachers. His job as he saw it was to tell them what to do. Their job was to do it; that's all he expected. However, he usually did not find it any easier to communicate with his neighbors. That sometimes worried him a little too. Though he often told himself he was not one to stand around and chat aimlessly, and they knew it. Respected him for it, he felt, and that, anyway, was as it should be.

"Turner," he supplied now. "One of the Indian family named Turner living in Douglas."

"Isn't there an Indian boy named Turner on your football team this year?"

"His brother. Benjamin." The name came promptly to the principal's tongue. With satisfaction. Knowing which name on his high school attendance list belonged to which student was a matter of importance to him. He remembered who Benjamin was very well.

"Well, they're all related more or less. This here young fellow who died probably graduated from your school."

Reluctantly, the principal had to admit he didn't really know. "They drop out, most of them, before they get to their senior year."

"Always been that way." John Onslatter was matter-of-fact. "Not much you can do about it."

"Something happens to them," the principal conceded. Teachers often talked about it at the faculty meetings.

There was a general feeling that it was a waste of time to pay much attention to Indian kids. In the three years Mr. Haley had been principal, only three had finished with the graduating class. Principal Haley had a tidy mind; in it was a ready store of facts and figures. Only three, he reflected. Benjamin Turner would be the fourth. The dropout rate among Indian students in the Douglas school was over 90 percent. He repeated the statistics to John with regretful significance.

"Funny thing," his father-in-law said suddenly. "Four is a kind of special number with Indians. Things happen at least four times in their stories, instead of always three like in ours."

Principal Haley had never heard that nor thought much about it before. Three bears, three little pigs, three blind mice, three wise men and three men in a tub. Three times were things cursed or blessed and three wishes were always granted. The principal went on musing. Jonah was in the belly of the whale three days and three nights and the Trinity was three. Certainly the rule was three. Always three. The principal nodded.

"Seems like with Indians, it's always been four."

Principal Haley smiled tolerantly and the two men gazed a moment out the camper window.

"Well, you graduated three of them so far. Maybe this Benjamin Turner will be Number Four."

Principal Haley didn't hear any portending drum sounds in his head. He was watching the white mist slithering down from the tall trees. Like the smoke of Indian fires billowing in the wind. It was only mist to him. He saw no thunderbird in the sky.

His answer was routine, automatic, and not even part of his thoughts. "Maybe, I certainly hope so."

Out the window, a thick liquid curtain was hanging straight down from the heavens. The same amount of rain any other place in the United States would be unbelievable, but not around Douglas. The wet built to as much as 140 inches a year, a sum of green. Green water rivers. Green moss. Green slopes falling into green meadows, full of wild game.

Hunting was the town of Douglas' own Olympian

game, as honored as the festival of ancient Greece. Tagging a deer was a crown of glory like a laurel wreath. The winners paraded all the way home, their bucks displayed across the car hoods. Sacrificial altars.

Principal Haley saw for an instant the Sears, Roebuck gun cabinet which stood in his own living room. A present from his father-in-law. The barrel and stock pits were lined in green felt; the doors were sliding glass — fine enough to show off old silver. Which only added to the principal's obligation for he had to purchase a rifle.

The school board members always gathered around the cabinet when they came to his house, as if it were the hearth place. It was a conversation piece, in the truer use of the phrase, a kind of credit card, really. Principal Haley was a conscientious host. He hung up coats, pulled up chairs, passed around cigars, laughed affably, agreed with everybody, and listened with attentive interest. No one thought to notice the absence of the principal's own hunting anecdotes.

"Dammit!" exploded the man across from him. "I can't help thinking about the one you missed."

Gregory Haley saw the deer's eyes again. Like newly dipped chocolates, still glistening. A perfect target. Head raised, hesitating. Frozen as a mountaintop. It was a young buck. And it looked at him with the trusting face of a papoose. He held his gun steadily, sighting between the eyes. Aimed — purposefully high — and fired. The miss had left his father-in-law gasping, speechless.

"By God, you'll never have as good a chance as that!" John Onslatter had finally spluttered. Gregory Haley silently hoped he never would.

The older man's sigh went whistling down before him. A tire with a slow puncture. A whish of wind come down through the trees. A lamentation. "Well, I guess you do your best."

Mr. Haley rolled the thought around in his mind. He savored the essential truth of it. As principal, he had never done anything less than his best. Indian or white made no difference to him. School rules were the same for all. No student, or teacher either, had ever given him any trouble.

Principal Haley fully expected to keep it that way.

3

Benjamin

BENJAMIN sat on the boat-haven dock at Salt Chuck squawking back at the sea gulls. The morning sky was still stormy. He was waiting for David.

The sea gulls screeched back at him. Going crazy in the wind. Liking it.

Some Saturday nights Benjamin slept overnight in Salt Chuck. This time he felt even more like a visitor. The storm woke him in the middle of the night. He lay awake listening to the beating and the banging, hoping it would keep up. Man! It was beautiful. Like his brother would say, the thunderbird and the whale were slamming it out together that night.

He got up too early to worry about waking anybody. The dirt road of the village was swept by the wind. The frozen ruts were hard and crusty beneath his boots.

It was pretty cold. The wind snapped at him. He zipped his parka up around his ears. His boots were thick-soled and cleated. The socks in them, wool. His shirt was warm flannel. And over it he wore his school-letter sweater. A big orange D on the left front. Football emblem and bars, and stripes on his sleeve. What David admired most were the stripes on Benjamin's sleeve. Next year he'd have three for senior.

Benjamin guessed there wasn't much left in him of the old-time Indian. It didn't bother him any. He didn't think Salt Chuck was much of an Indian village. It was only a remnant. A leftover. Almost a fossil.

One weekend each summer the villagers became "real" Indians again. They dressed up in deerskin garments trimmed with porcupine quills. They put on head masks made of painted cedar, or headdresses of eagle feathers. They sold Indian baskets, and baked salmon lashed to sticks, Indian style. Dugout canoes raced in the river, and drums beat for Indian dances. But Benjamin never felt any part of it. He felt more like a tourist.

Benjamin walked up and down for a while. He kept waiting for David.

The tourist cabins under the hemlocks on the ocean beach were empty. No charter boats were going out. And none were coming in. All that was left were Indian dugout canoes. Waterlogged. Summertime the sound of their outboard motors came chopping across the reservation.

That was one of the crazy things he and David argued about. Whether echoes kept going on right through winter.

"Sure they do," his brother would insist. "You can hear them if you listen."

"How do you mean, listen?"

"Like an Indian."

Benjamin listened for about three seconds. Then he said, "I don't hear anything."

But his brother sat there all solemn like a mummy. A cigar-store Indian. He wondered whether David really believed in all the things he talked about. Old Indian stuff. Like spirit power and songs.

"You're not trying," his brother said.

"Sure I'm trying. I can't help it if I've grown out of my Indian costume." He grinned, rather fancying the idea of that. If he had his free choice, he'd cast it off. Like a shirt too short at the wrists.

"Apple!" his brother would throw at him. It meant red on the outside. Like an Indian. But white on the inside.

That was supposed to make Benjamin mad. But it didn't. Actually, he was rather pleased that David had noticed it. Benjamin had noticed it himself long ago. He had even hoped that if he got white enough on the inside it might someday carry all the way out.

"You are one crazy Indian!" David had said then.

He said that all the time. *You are one crazy Indian.*

Benjamin decided to listen for the echoes. He figured David couldn't be wrong all the time. So he listened.

He heard the tattooing of his heart. He heard the seawater roiling beyond the jetty. And maybe the sound of whales singing. He heard the mooing of the foghorn on the point. But no echoes. They were still back there somewhere. Caught maybe in the closed-up tourist cabins. Locked inside the empty charter boats.

Winter had no echoes, Benjamin decided. Not in Salt Chuck anyway. Salt Chuck was like a theater with the stage empty. A car run out of gas. A pot with nothing boiling. Winter in Salt Chuck was only television antennas sticking out of thick gray mist.

Benjamin began answering back to the gulls again. It gave him something to do. It kept him warm. He also inspected a gill net, set in an eddy. One end was tied to a tree on the bank. The other end was anchored in the quieter water of the river.

Once in a while there would be a big steelhead trapped in it by its gills. Its head would be stuck through the mesh like a cow caught in a fence. A steelhead was a large rainbow trout. It came back to the river to spawn. Like a salmon. Except a steelhead didn't die after it spawned. It went back out to sea again.

Salt Chuck Indians were gillnetters. They used to be whalers, David said. Long ago. Pretty soon they'd be buying all their fish at the store. That's what Benjamin always told David. When he wanted to start a good argument.

He and his brother argued a lot. They'd sit on the boat-haven float hollering at each other. They argued about a lot of things.

Benjamin hardly ever argued with Harold. They were friends. Not brothers. Anyway they didn't seem to have so much to argue about. Harold didn't have opinions. They just did things together. Like going to school. And racing in a car up and down the main street of Douglas. And drinking beer. Or camping down on the beach overnight.

When they talked, it was about things that happened at school. Who might be a good candidate for president of the senior class (Benjamin). Who would talk the coach into getting them a pass to the State college football game (Benjamin). Who would invite the girls to go to a show and arrange to meet them inside (Benjamin). Who'd get to sit in the back seat when they parked with girls and who had to go down to the beach — well maybe they did argue about that. But he'd usually let Harold win. Because David always let Benjamin win.

Pretty soon David would come caroming up the village road in his red Toyota. He'd come walking with long steps down the long finger of the dock with his transistor radio going loud. Maybe he'd have a couple of cans of beer in his back pocket. Maybe it would be a carton of milk.

"What you got to do," David would start out telling him, "is keep going to school. Whatever happens, just keep going. Because let me tell you, you're no 'dumb Injun.' When you graduate high school, you go to college. And when you get out of college, you'll have your eyes open. You'll tell the white man things he doesn't even know about. He will look amazed and think to himself, 'Man, this guy has really got something on the ball.' And pretty soon he'll be thinking, 'I'd better be careful because this Injun Benjamin may get ahead of me!' "

Benjamin sat there by himself and laughed out loud. Like crazy. Then he heard the sound of feet. He swung around. It was his father coming along the plankway.

Benjamin wondered what his father had come all the way out to Salt Chuck for. He stood up, waiting.

The wet wind slapped at his face. It pressed like ice on his bare forehead. Suddenly another kind of cold grabbed his heart.

He knew about his brother David. Even before his father began to tell him.

4

A Killing

PLASTIC FLOWERS bloomed brightly on the hill behind the village. The flowers in the vases looked real at first, but the trees around did not. They wore shrouds of mist. Benjamin walked lightly over the grasses in the old Indian cemetery. The graves lay, turned every which way. People lying all over the beach on a hot day. Soldiers fallen where they had stood on the battlefield.

There was a broken bedspring there. Old and rusted. Probably long ago the bedsprings had been "killed" so they could "die" with their owner and go with him to the land of the dead. But nobody believed in doing things like that anymore. Benjamin turned away.

Indians believed they crossed a river when they died. Once, his mother had told him of a Salt Chuck Indian named Joe Barber who fell sick and died. But two days later, when he was about to be buried, he came back to life. He had gone to the land of the dead, he said, and come back.

He told everyone that the road to the land of the dead was narrow and winding. Like the road to Salt Chuck. At first he didn't know where he was or where he was going. Finally, he came to a river. Like the river at Salt Chuck. Across the river he saw people walking about. Nobody paid any attention to him at first. Then an old lady came down to the river on the other side. She called to him to come across and he saw it was his mother. That was when he realized that this was the land of the dead. But he was sure he wasn't dead. So he turned around and walked back. Everybody thought it was lucky that Joe Barber came back before they buried him.

Benjamin had laughed at the story.

The Indian belief was that the dead could come back if they really wanted to. But Benjamin hadn't ever known anyone who did. Maybe they didn't want to come back. He guessed David wouldn't — even if he could.

David had always wanted to make things. But he wasn't very good at it. He didn't know how to fix things any better than he knew how to make things.

Once he had tried to make a dugout canoe. Benjamin

grinned. Even long ago there were hardly two Indians to a village who could really do a good job making a canoe. In Salt Chuck now there weren't any.

A canoe had to be made from one log, split down the middle. The log not only had to be hollowed out, but shaped and curved. You had to have a good eye and a good hand. Canoe makers had to have a special kind of ability.

David said the reason they were good canoe makers was because they had spirit power. David was strong on spirit power. He really believed it. He was always looking for some himself.

Once he had gone off and stayed in the forest by himself for four days. But evidently that was not long enough. He saw no vision or heard no song and when he grew hungry he just came home.

He thought the reason he wasn't very good at anything was that he had never found any kind of spirit power. Not for making canoes, or catching fish, or playing baseball, or hunting deer, or even fixing cars. He tried all the different ways he had ever heard of to find himself some spirit power. But he never found any, no matter what he did.

If any power ever came to him, he said, Benjamin would surely know. Because if he got it, he'd get it strong. Some got it so strong they started running like crazy. They'd hurl themselves against houses or trees or into the sea. One Indian who got his power burst a hole right through the wall of his house. David knew because he saw the hole.

Benjamin laughed. If it happened in Douglas no one would believe it was power. Everyone would just say the 'dumb Injun' was drunk.

Spirit power sometimes came with a song. You didn't have to learn the tune or words to it. All you had to do was open your mouth, and it came out. Ever after that, your song was your own personal property. Like your hat or your shoes. Singing it helped make your power work for you. No Indian ever talked much about his power, though. It could fade away if it was talked about. Anyway that's what Indians believed.

Benjamin didn't. Not any of it.

He closed his eyes and held himself very still. He saw David walking again along the plankway to the boat haven. He could almost hear the blast of David's transistor radio. David wouldn't want to go anywhere without his radio.

Benjamin headed back down the hill fast. Partly because he was in a hurry, partly for fun. He liked driving fast. He felt like a thunderbird himself when he was swooping along the road in his car. The flash of his eyes was lightning. He could make thunder roll or rain come — if he went fast enough. But he never could go fast enough.

He raced all the way home to get David's radio.

But he drove slowly back. He wasn't sure why he did,

he just did. Maybe because he was feeling kind of silly.
He didn't really believe in any of the old Indian stuff.
He never had, he reminded himself, as he reached the
little graveyard on top of the hill again.

Benjamin laid the radio on the new grave. He set it
next to the blue vase of plastic flowers. Yellow and
white. Permanently blooming. But somehow the radio
didn't look right stuck in the dirt there.

Benjamin rubbed his hands over its smooth case. He
turned it on letting it blare a rock tune. Automatically
he snapped his fingers to its beat. David liked that one.
He listened for a while. The singing screeched over the
graveyard on the hill, a bird inside a tin can.

Then he did it. He killed it. Hitting it against a rock
until the plastic case cracked and the music stopped. He
shook it. Nothing rattled inside. Dead.

Benjamin lifted his head listening. He heard the faint
sound of the surf, a kind of music too. But he didn't
hear any "You are one crazy Indian."

He stared at the broken radio in his hand, feeling
foolish.

"Man! You are one crazy Indian!" he said in imitation
of David's voice.

But he left the broken radio behind him in the graveyard for David.

5

Indians

PRINCIPAL HALEY didn't know exactly when he began to feel a certain disquiet. It was some time after he had shot at the deer and missed it. A good many weeks after that day on which Benjamin's brother, David, had been found dead.

It began like a gentle steaming in the teakettle before the water begins to bubble. The kind of thing that sometimes starts as a minor annoyance — an itch on the elbow, or a tiny pimple on the back of the neck — and grows unwarranted into a flaming sore. Pinpricks of discomfort, here and there, that combine to wake you up one morning with a booming migraine.

Certainly no one thing of any real significance occurred during the remainder of that school year. At least, taken by itself, each seemed totally unrelated to the others and trifling. Too small to be important.

One day in the early spring, the Indian children came to school on the yellow bus dressed in tribal ceremonial costume. With only a little surprise and mild discomfiture, Mr. Haley viewed the solemn procession of children as they stepped off the bus. No permission for any such display had been asked or granted. Of course, strictly speaking, there were no dress-conformity rules at the Douglas school. The students wore what they preferred so long as it was decent.

The Indian children walked solemnly to their classes, as if they had been dressed as usual. Among the white students there was considerable snickering, and one of the teachers was quite upset. The principal guessed she feared an uprising of some sort, and perhaps underneath he entertained that thought for a moment, too. Ridiculous, of course.

Only the kindergarten teacher seemed perfectly delighted. She came running to ask his permission to have them all march through the primary grade rooms to show off their costumes. The art teacher took their picture. At the end of the day the Indian children climbed, as usual, back into their bus and returned to the reservation.

That's all there was to it. Indian Day, they called it. It was nothing, he reported in a confident voice to the superintendent, but he was not really sure. Benjamin Turner was absent that day.

Principal Haley made a careful check of the recent attendance records. Benjamin Turner had been absent a number of times. Not unusual when one considered the high absence rate among Indian students in the high school. Yet it was inconsistent with his previous record.

Then there was the matter of parking. Benjamin's small car was more often than not parked in the faculty parking zone. A small thing perhaps.

Mr. Haley, in genuine kindness, warned him several times. The boy was always polite and seemed sincerely surprised. He had not paid any attention to where he had parked, he said, as if his mind had been traveling other roads. Certainly not an unusual state of mind for most eighteen-year-old boys. Was it for this one? The principal touched on the question in his mind but he really didn't know.

When Benjamin Turner was nominated for class president the principal couldn't in all good conscience permit him to run. He held firm in denying Benjamin any special privilege.

"Rules are rules," he said. Benjamin had been absent from school too often without adequate excuses, and he had persistently ignored the parking prohibitions. No student who had violations against his record was eligible for a class office.

A noisy group of supporters protested. He told them gravely, "If I make an exception for one candidate, I would have to make exceptions for all."

There had been small ripples among the teaching staff,

too. Mr. Otis, the biology teacher, was not making himself at all popular among the lady teachers in the teachers' lounge. He left his cigarettes burning. He used anybody's coffee cup. He spoke up too challengingly on what he called faculty blind spots.

Mr. Haley noted that he was outspoken at the teachers' meetings too. Like a ball slipping out of his grasp, the focus seemed too often to bounce over to Mr. Otis. The biology teacher was baldly critical of other teachers. When he referred to the Indian students attending the school, he made a formal body out of them. They were "the Indian Minority." Mr. Haley ignored most of it until he began to suspect that Indian Day might have walked right out of Mr. Otis' head.

He noted that Benjamin Turner was often in Mr. Otis' room between classes, talking with him, or maybe listening, but so were others. Mr. Otis was a popular teacher — especially with the Indian students.

Mr. Haley could put his finger on nothing that was exactly untoward.

He made a point of stepping up his informal inspections of Mr. Otis' class, walking past the windows on the outside several times a day, looking in at the door, going in to listen for a moment.

He returned to his office after a tour of such official observance one afternoon to find visitors. A committee of interested citizens waited to see him. Did he know that some of his students were freely, too freely in the committee's opinion, going in and out of a house across the street from the school?

The house was rented. The tenant's hair was thick and suspiciously long. His mustache framed his mouth or concealed the lower part of his face, depending on how you looked at it. He lived half the time at Salt Chuck and he spent a lot of time with Indians. The visitors weren't sure how he earned his living though they thought he was a fisherman. The kids called him Leo, not even Mr., just Leo.

Principal Haley made notes on his pad of paper as he listened dutifully. He thanked them for making him aware of the situation and he ushered them out without promising anything. Their concern was natural.

There was nothing to it, of course.

He walked out of the school at 4:30 P.M. with the problem on his mind. He nodded to one or two people on his way to the main street corner.

He stopped at the barber shop, and sat there waiting his turn, his coat still neatly buttoned up, his leather gloves tucked into his pocket, his felt hat set on the seat of the chair beside him.

"Be with you in a minute!"

He opened the page of the newspaper.

"Terrible thing at Kent State," the barber said over his clippers. "Shooting kids like that."

"Their own fault," said the man in the chair. His heavy boots stuck out from under the edge of the striped apron. His Mackinaw hung on a wall hook behind the principal's chair. Mr. Haley stood up, removed his own coat, folded it and laid it down beside him.

"Too much of that all over now," said the other customer. "Outsiders come in and get the kids organized. Work 'em up. It's not a safe job being president of a university anymore. Look what's happening in California at Berkeley. Riots all over the campus. It's catching, it is. Some of the kids in the high schools around the country are doing the same thing. Before you know it, the whole country will go smash."

"Well, there's a lot to this civil rights," said the barber. "Isn't that right, Principal?"

Principal Haley smiled, a futile attempt. His face felt stiff and grim. "There's a lot in what you say," he said, and decided not to wait for a haircut.

That night he was restless. His father-in-law called him up in the middle of the night for something or other. He couldn't remember what it was about the next morning.

At school, he noted all at once that the Indian students always seemed to walk down the halls with their heads down. They never looked you in the eye when you spoke to them.

Principal Haley sat in his office most of the day making thoughtful notations on a neat square of paper. He kept trying to add everything up in his mind. But there didn't seem to be any logical answer that way. He tried reversing the process. Reducing each item to its simplest common denominator. Trying to find some element all the pieces shared. And the answer he came up with gave him a little start. It was — Indian.

Uneasily, he reflected that less than a century ago the inhabitants of the nearby village of Salt Chuck were whale-hunting, fish-eating natives, naked or dressed in skins or shredded bark, and armed with spears or bow and arrow.

Ridiculous! Principal Haley allowed himself a hearty laugh and dismissed his conclusion perforce. It was fanciful. He put it out of his mind.

But his fourth year as school principal began and an apprehension stayed with him. He was aware of it hiding in the back of his mind. Like a bogyman in a closet.

6

Who Are You?

MR. OTIS' FACE was sort of round and fat. His hair hung over his forehead and licked at his eyes. His glasses had thick square rims, and when he fixed his glance on you, his eyeballs were shiny as fish eggs. He talked fast and loud and when he got really excited he moved back and forth from one foot to the other.

To the biology teacher sex wasn't a dirty word. As far as words were concerned, obscenity was all "bunko" to him.

"There are no dirty words," Mr. Otis said to his class. Half-lidded eyes opened. Heads came up. Twitching bottoms sat fast, glued suddenly to their seats. And Harold Slater, who usually fell asleep in any class that followed lunch, sat up. "Unless you want to make them that way."

Even the ones in the class who preferred doing assignments to rapping with Mr. Otis paid attention. Sometimes Mr. Otis made them think. Even when they didn't want to.

"In some communities *black* is a dirty word," Mr. Otis said. Then he said — "*Red* happens to be the dirty word in some others."

Benjamin tried to separate himself by looking out the window. But that didn't do much good. All he saw was the yellow bus that carried the Indian kids to school every day. Dust was thick on its backside. Someone's finger had traced on its side, *You're an Indian.*

Red—the Indians didn't think about being "Indians" when they were in Salt Chuck. The only place Indians really felt like "Indians" was in Douglas.

Benjamin pinched his finger where his class ring had been. He had given it to his girl. He hadn't thought about her not being an Indian.

They sat together on the white side in the Douglas movie theater. There was no rule against that anymore. But most of the Indians still shuffled over to the Indian side.

Benjamin saw the principal walking past the windows. Like he didn't have anything else to do. Slow enough to look in.

The principal frowned. Probably at the stuff sitting on the tables. Or the things hanging on the walls. Benjamin looked at the calendar. All scrawled up. Like the yellow bus.

Mr. Haley liked to see chairs in straight rows. He thought students should raise their hands when they wanted to say something. He thought they should not stack their books on the floor. He thought a teacher shouldn't allow everybody to write all over his calendar.

Nothing like that bothered Mr. Otis. He didn't believe in tests. Or in writing out a lot of papers. He called all that "bunko." He talked to Indian students the same way he talked to whites.

Mr. Otis stopped talking suddenly. He looked out the window and waved at Principal Haley. It made the principal move quickly on, as if he had just forgotten something.

Mr. Otis didn't even give the class a chance to laugh. He went on talking. He pulled at his ear sometimes while he talked. He moved around a lot. Like a gnat. Or a sand crab running backward on the shore. Climbing over some rocks and under others. Poking and pulling at things. Mr. Otis poked and pulled at Benjamin's mind.

Your mind was like an oyster to Mr. Otis. He tried to drop a grain of sand into it. It irritated. But that's what made it grow a pearl. Mr. Otis was always saying things like that. Half the time, no one knew what he was talking about. Benjamin always had to think about it awhile first.

Mr. Otis thought the high school kids should do more thinking. He thought they should talk up about things, too. He got all excited talking about how much more the kids should be talking. He was a pretty big talker all by himself.

Benjamin liked to listen to Mr. Otis. But when he really wanted to talk, he talked to Leo. He hardly ever went out to Salt Chuck anymore. Instead he went over to Leo's.

Leo's house had an old davenport in the living room and not many chairs. A coffeepot was always heating on the kitchen burner. A big drawing of an old sailing vessel with high masts covered practically one wall. Leo had three guitars and lots of hi-fi stereo components sitting around. His kitchen cupboards were full of tapes and records. He played music loud. Loud enough to drown out any thought you didn't feel like thinking. They talked a lot.

One day Leo had taken Benjamin with him to Seattle. The city lay like an octopus. Spreading out into a bay, and between a couple of lakes and a river. Its streets and sidewalks ran up and down hills, and from the top of any, your head was in the clouds. "Not exactly a paradise," Leo said. To Benjamin it seemed pretty close to it. He decided he would go to the university there when he graduated from high school.

Another time they had gone back together to see a play called *Indians*. It was all about Buffalo Bill. Benjamin and David had done a lot of laughing about Buffalo Bill. Some big hero! Buffalo Bill.

On the way home they had a couple of beers and

Benjamin started to cry. Only he didn't know what he was crying about. It didn't matter to Leo. He seemed to know.

Benjamin began to listen to Mr. Otis. He watched Mr. Otis rear end as he crossed the room.

"Who are you?" Mr. Otis said suddenly, whirling around. "You." He pointed. "And you. And you!"

"Who, me?" Harold Slater's grin was beautiful. Everyone knew who Harold was. His father owned the biggest logging mill in the area. His mother's grandfather was a pioneer.

An early settler was a kingpin in Douglas. A first-stringer. A four-star general. Chairman of the board and top of the heap. Everybody knew who Harold was all right. He was pure cream and all white.

An article about Harold's family was in the newspaper regularly once a year. Sometimes even twice. Two columns of bravery, strength and determination. With pictures of what the area looked like eighty years ago. Elk trails. Rivers that raged with rains. Miles of lonely ocean beach. Threatening forests of cougar, coyote, bobcat, and bear. And wild Indians. Most of the teachers in the Douglas school still saw them as wild Indians. They were still thinking they had to "tame" them instead of teach them.

Benjamin laughed. But the noise didn't bother Mr. Otis any.

"Who are you?" Mr. Otis said again, looking at Benjamin.

The bell rang, and everybody started banging books and getting up. Mr. Otis went on talking. Softly. Talking straight to Benjamin.

"When you find out who you are, you'll be able to function better in this white world."

Benjamin picked up his books.

They had really tamed him, he guessed. All his life he had been busy learning how to be a white man. He had never stopped to ask himself, "Who am I?"

7

Retain White Copy,
Return Pink Copy with Reply

FROM: Gregory E. Haley, Principal
To: Mr. Lloyd Otis
SUBJECT: Early dismissal of class

*Will you please keep your fourth period class in session
until the bell rings at 12:20 p.m.*
DATE: December 20, 1970

* * *

FROM: Gregory E. Haley, Principal
To: Mr. Lloyd Otis
SUBJECT: Security of Room 201

*At 4:00 p.m. I found two windows unsecured in Room
201 and your room door was unlocked. Also, today your
room door was not locked during your conference period.
When checking your room yesterday afternoon, I found*

a microscope left in the proximity of one of the unlocked windows.

DATE: January 3, 1971

* * *

FROM: Gregory E. Haley, Principal
TO: Mr. Lloyd Otis
SUBJECT: Student movement, regulations of

Today I noticed two incidents during seventh period which were not in accord with our rules regarding students entering and departing classes.

A girl entered your class and sought the attention of another student immediately upon entering the room. The girl's voice was loud and I am sure it was disruptive and, secondly, she did not seek your permission to be in your class. A boy left your class without permission or slip and went to the art room. Will you keep a closer check on your student's or students' movement?

DATE: January 15, 1971

* * *

FROM: Gregory E. Haley, Principal
TO: Mr. Lloyd Otis
SUBJECT: State of cleanliness of Island Sinks in Room 201

At 9:00 a.m. February 11, 1971, I checked your room and found the island sinks in a below-standard condition.

Sinks were cluttered with peanut shells, gum wrappers, etc., and also the enclosed areas below the sinks were not in acceptable condition. Will you please remedy this condition as soon as possible?
DATE: February 12, 1971

* * *

FROM: Gregory E. Haley, Principal
TO: Mr. Lloyd Otis
SUBJECT: Window shades

On the item of drawn shades in your room. I would prefer that you seek some other way in which to combat your objection to the open shades.
DATE: February 15, 1971

* * *

8

The Game

THE WINDOW SHADES were up again, Benjamin noted. The window shades were up and the biology teacher was busy with the saltwater aquarium. It needed cleaning, but Mr. Otis wasn't doing that.

In front of the room, a bunch of girls stood giggling. Someone threw an eraser at them. Mr. Otis looked up but it didn't bother him. It landed on the floor below the window.

Outside, the principal came by, walking fast. But he didn't stop to look in. He just hurried past.

Mr. Otis smiled. He didn't mind poking fun at the principal. Or anyone else for that matter. Mr. Otis called himself a free soul.

A lot had been going on between Mr. Otis and the principal lately. Benjamin hadn't paid too much attention. He hadn't been at school much. He had been taking off. By himself. Driving his car down to the beach or up the mountain road. Thinking.

Principal Haley had called him in again to talk about that. He had lectured him on skipping school. He was okay about it though. He said he'd let it go this time without any disciplinary action. Just so Benjamin would promise not to let it happen again. He didn't even notice that Benjamin didn't open his mouth to promise anything. Not anything at all.

"Prejudice," said Mr. Otis. "I think it's about time that we discuss the nature of prejudice. In a scientific way. Because everybody thinks he knows what it means."

"I don't know what it means," Byron Hill called out. He was trying to be funny. Byron's idea of being funny was writing stuff on Mr. Otis' calendar, or following a girl right up to the door of the Girls'. Teachers were always giving him notes to take to other teachers. His father was on the school board.

Mr. Otis smiled as if he. had said something really bright. He was delighted, for some reason.

"Okay," said Mr. Otis. "Let's demonstrate." Mr. Otis was big on demonstrations.

"Prejudice is something you have to feel to know. Right?"

"If you say so," said Byron. He said things like that all the time.

Mr. Otis went to his desk and pulled open a drawer. He took out a bunch of paper, and started ripping. He

ripped several sheets at a time. Into strips. He made a
big pile of short strips and a little pile of long strips.

Then he turned the wastebasket upside down into
the sink. He left all gum wrappers, crumpled papers and
pencil shavings in the sink and set the wastebasket on
his desk. Then he dropped the strips of paper into the
wastebasket and stirred them around.

"All who want to take part in this demonstration, come
on up here."

Byron shrugged and moved slowly forward. He put
his hand into the basket and drew out one of the short
strips. A couple of girls came up together, giggling.
They pulled out short strips too. Mr. Otis stirred the
papers around some more.

Benjamin got himself up and pulled out a strip —
short. The next pulled out was long. And the next. And
the next. Soon the whole class stood around the room,
the torn slips in their hands.

"Okay," said Mr. Otis sharply. A top sergeant direct-
ing his recruits. "All you holding the long slips are INS.
For demonstration purposes today that stands for Indians. The short slips are the OUTS."

"What does that stand for?" someone asked.

Mr. Otis only smiled.

"All the INS automatically get A's today. All the
OUTS get D's."

The class groaned.

"Hey! I want to be an Indian!"

That brought laughs.

Mr. Otis pushed his hair back off his forehead. He grinned. "Everyone will have an assignment today," he announced. "The assignment is to read Chapter Four from *The Human Zoo* by Desmond Morris. There are three paperback copies in the library. I put them there myself. That's all there are, so you will have to do your research there."

He looked around the room with a broad smile. A cherub in thick square glasses.

"But what's the use of doing the assignment if you are an OUT. Like you said — I'll only get a D anyway."

"Right!" said Mr. Otis, looking even more pleased. "That's the nature of prejudice. Now you're learning what it's all about!"

Somebody laughed. A little shakily.

"By the way," said Mr. Otis. "Anyone who doesn't do the assignment will get an F for failure. With his name posted on the bulletin board." He added, "All grades will be posted there."

"In the hall?"

"That's right. In the front hall."

"But my mother is coming to a PTA meeting tomorrow. She'll see it."

Mr. Otis shrugged. "That's the nature of prejudice."

There was a sudden complete silence in the room. Like at a party when everyone stops talking accidentally at the same time. The aquarium gurgled. Like a man strangling.

Two of the OUTS began comparing their slips. "Hey!" said one. "My slip is longer than his!"

"But it's not as long as mine," said a girl proudly.

"It's three-quarters as long."

"So is mine!" said someone else.

Mr. Otis pursed his lips, examining the slips. It was true. Carelessly torn, some shorter slips were almost twice as long as others. Though not as long as the longest.

"Okay," he conceded. "I will permit all those with three-quarter slips to be three-quarter Indians. But if you are not at least three-quarter Indian, you are not permitted to use the library."

There was a frantic huddling in the center of the room. All those with short slips noisily compared one with the other.

Benjamin sat, and watched. They were really all excited, he thought. They were really acting as if they had to prove they were at least three-quarter Indian. He grinned.

"Mr. Otis! Mr. Otis! Can an IN nominate an OUT to be voted in?"

Mr. Otis blinked his eyes a moment considering. He chuckled. "Maybe so. Let's say — an OUT can become an IN by a unanimous vote."

There was a sigh of relief from two girls. They were huddled together like two sandpipers adrift on a log.

"BUT" — Mr. Otis' finger pointed warningly into the air —"All OUTS voted in have to wait until all original INS finish their assignment in the library before they are allowed to enter. Remember, OUTS. Even should you be voted IN you are still only a second-class citizen!"

He looked at his watch, then opened the door. "Now there is still a half hour of the period left. All INS may depart to the library. Any OUTS with a hope of being voted in may go with them."

The classroom door stayed open. They could easily hear the discussion in the hall in front of the library door. They heard arguing. The girl who had held onto the hand of her friend wanted all to vote on her right then. Some wouldn't agree until they had gotten to the books first.

For a moment then all was quiet. Then the principal's voice was heard echoing through the hall.

"Young lady. What are you doing here?"

"I'm waiting to go into the library."

"Is it closed?"

She must have shaken her head.

"Then — I don't see — "

"Oh, I'm not permitted to go in," she said.

"And to whom do you owe this restriction?"

"Mr. Otis."

"May I ask why Mr. Otis does not permit you to enter the library?"

"It's because I'm not three-quarters Indian," she said.

With a grin, Mr. Otis closed the classroom door.

9

The Indian Culture Club

BENJAMIN TURNER is here to see you," the office clerk said. "Again." He had been in three times that week already.

"It's been a busy week," the principal said. "Tell Benjamin to wait. Or come back later."

"I'll wait," said Benjamin. He sat down on a polished chair. He looked out the window and saw the yellow bus arriving from Salt Chuck.

He smelled its insides again. Its fragrance came to his nose like an old echo to his ear. He had come to school on the bus in the first grade. Then they had moved into the trailer in Douglas. The first thing Benjamin learned in Douglas was that Indian was a compound word. The first half of it was *dumb*. DumbIndian.

"*My mother says I'm not supposed to sit next to an Indian.*"

"Yah! What do you know — you're only an Indian!"

"Go back to the reservation where you belong!"

School for most Indian kids was a bad experience right from the first grade.

Indians think that staring at a person straight in the eyes is an insult to him.

But at school the teacher said, "Look at me when I speak to you!"

The teacher asked an Indian a question and he'd think about it. Looking away like Indians do.

"Well, sit down, we know you can't answer it!" the teacher said loudly.

The non-Indians laughed at him.

Making fun of someone is the Indian way of punishing. Indians laugh at anyone in their village who does wrong. When an Indian kid does something bad, his parents will say, "Shame, everybody will laugh at you." An Indian kid would rather be skinned alive than to have people laugh at him.

Going to school in Douglas, the Indian kids felt they were being punished all the time. Some of them walked down the halls with their heads hanging down right from the start. When they got to the fifth or sixth grade, some of them were walking around that way all the time.

When the Indian students acted differently than the whites, the teachers thought that proved how dumb they were.

Most of the Indian kids from Salt Chuck went to

school in Douglas only as long as they had to. Sometimes an Indian goes and sits in the class but he's not really there. He goes away. Like Indians do when they don't like you. Or think you are interfering. He goes as far away as he can and still be sitting in the class.

That makes him seem all the dumber to the teacher.

The Indian parents will stop making him go to school after a while. They know what's been happening. It happened to them in the same way.

It happened to David.

White time was different from Indian time. White jokes were different from Indian jokes. White people valued different things. They acted in different ways.

"I don't even think of you as an Indian" was supposed to be a compliment. *"If I don't think of you as an Indian, I can like you. But when I think of you as an Indian, I can't"* was what it meant.

Benjamin looked at the closed door to the principal's office.

If the Indian students could form a club at school, he thought, they could meet like any other club and look at their problems together.

With their own club the Indian students would feel like they were a part of the school too.

Maybe they could even begin to change the whole false idea most of the teachers and students had of Indians.

At their meetings they could talk about their Indian

culture. And how to deal with it. They could participate in school activities as a club in the way the other clubs did. Maybe there wouldn't be as many Indian dropouts if they had a club. A club for Indians would give them an identity. They could call it the Indian Culture Club.

The office clerk smiled at him. "Nothing critical, I hope?"

Benjamin gazed over her head thoughtfully. "Well, it's a matter of identity."

"Oh."

White people who don't understand what you're talking about usually say, "Oh," Benjamin had noticed.

He decided he would ask Mr. Haley about planning a field trip as soon as the club got organized. School clubs got to use the school buses for field trips. Their Indian Culture Club might sponsor a trip to the ancient Indian dig on the Cape. Its discovery had been in all the newspapers. The Indian kids could go all together and see how their ancestors lived 500 — maybe even a thousand years ago. Nobody knew yet how far back it went. They hadn't even gotten down to the lowest level.

It would be a great beginning for the Douglas High School Indian Culture Club.

With their own Indian Culture Club, the Indian students could begin to get back their self-respect at school. They could begin to find their pride again.

The door to the principal's office opened.

"What's on your mind, Benjamin?"

"The Indian Culture Club."

"Oh."

"I've been over to the college again. They've got one going over there. They said they'd send someone to explain things and help us get going. And I talked to Mr. Otis too. He said he'd be the adviser."

"Mr. Otis? Was this his idea?"

"It's my idea," Benjamin said honestly. "An Indian club for Indian students only. That's the whole idea of it. Non-Indians not allowed."

Principal Haley nodded.

"I have not forgotten. Other matters have taken my attention. Critical matters," he added.

"This is pretty important too. To Indians."

The principal looked at him. A little oddly, Benjamin thought.

"Sit down, Benjamin."

Benjamin sat down.

"Now let me see if I understand it correctly. Your proposed club will be only for Indians."

"A culture club," said Benjamin. "For Indians only. We want to talk about our own culture, the Indian culture. We want to rap about our problems. Have a real organization."

"Well, I'm afraid it is against the rules for any club or organization of a discriminatory nature to form on schooltime and under school auspices."

"Discriminatory?!"

"Since your Indian club will not include whites, it is therefore — discriminatory. We cannot allow the formation of an all-Indian culture club any more than we could allow an all-white culture club. The rules are clear. It wouldn't be fair."

"But the white kids don't need any all-white culture club."

"I've gone into this quite extensively, Benjamin — "

"But we aren't talking about the same thing, Mr. Haley."

"I'm talking about this, Benjamin. As long as I am principal of this school, I will go by the rules. I cannot allow any group that excludes others because this is discrimination itself. No Indian group can exclude whites. Nor can any white group exclude Indians. Not here in the Douglas school."

"But you've got to see the difference!"

The principal unwound his fingers and tapped a little impatiently with his fingernails on the top of the desk. He looked at his watch. "I'm afraid I see no difference at all, Benjamin."

He opened the door for Benjamin and closed it firmly behind him.

In the outer office, Benjamin stared down at the top of the counter. The attendance list lay open there. The names of all the students were there in alphabetical order. Neatly typed. Precisely columned. You could see who was in school at a glance. Only occasional red checks marred the orderly black and white of the long pages. The red-marked names popped out at Benjamin. Warren Black, Diana Holt. He swept to the next page. Benjamin Turner. A red X was next to his name. He looked quickly up and down the open pages. Each and every Indian student attending Douglas Junior and Senior High School was identified by a red X at the left of his name. The red X was for Indian. *DumbIndian.*

"He'd like to help you," the office clerk said with a worried look. "But he has to be fair. Principal Haley always leans over backward to be impartial and fair."

Benjamin flipped the attendance book shut and walked out.

10

Canoes, Baskets and Totems

$\mathbf{M}$R. HALEY was standing outside his office door when Benjamin came into the school building. "Oh, Benjamin!" Mr. Haley called out to him.

There was a warm smile on Mr. Haley's face. He led Benjamin into his office.

"I believe I have something that will interest you."

Benjamin set his books on the floor below his chair. "The Indian Culture Club?"

"Well, it concerns Indian culture all right," the principal said. Like a pat on the head. "I've ordered some audio-visual materials on Indians. Mr. Kerry happened to bring it to my attention. Beautiful stuff according to the literature sent out on it. Slides and transparencies. There's a great one on Indian designs showing Indian baskets and another on totem poles and one on canoes."

The principal sat back with a pleased expression on his face. "Now what I thought — seeing your interest in helping your people to know more about themselves — is to let you take it over as your own project. Extracurricular so to speak. You can get the whole thing set up yourself. Include as much of it as you want and prepare a showing for the seventh-graders. Perhaps you can get it ready for an assembly — say in May?"

Benjamin sat there.

"Well, Benjamin, you've been in and out of my office a lot lately talking about pride and about dignity and learning more about Indian culture and it seems to me this audio-visual thing will do exactly what you want to do."

Mr. Haley began moving the things around on his desk. Still smiling. Still pleased with himself. "You're a capable boy, Benjamin. There's good stuff in you. You need a little direction, of course. And this could be a worthwhile endeavor for you. Why, Mr. Kerry was very excited about the quality of this film. Said there were some beautiful shots of carvings. Said the totem poles were extraordinary. Beautiful design work! All in color. Now what do you say?"

Benjamin stared at the inkwell on Mr. Haley's desk. It was an old-fashioned one. Then he saw it was one designed to only look like an old-fashioned inkwell. A quill pen was stuck into a holder next to it. Not the real thing. It had a ball point.

"About the Indian Culture Club," Benjamin began. Mr. Haley wasn't listening. The Indian Culture Club was a closed subject, Benjamin could see. The Indian project looked enough like it to Mr. Haley. The Indian project was the substitute.

"Well, think about it some more, Benjamin," the principal said. "I've spent a good deal of my time on this already. It seems like a very good thing to me. I hope I've given you something to think about, too."

Benjamin stood up. "Man, you've given me something to think about all right," he said.

His girl, Louise Barry, was hanging around outside the door. "Hi," she said. "I thought I saw you go in here. You been talking to the principal again?"

"He does all the talking," said Benjamin. "He never listens to Indians."

She said mildly, "Well you've been going in and out of there a lot lately."

He plowed along beside her. A jam of students filled the hallway. Louise hung on to his arm. He saw his ring on her finger. He looked at it without any special feeling. She was not an Indian. He didn't expect her to understand.

11

Crazy Indian

It surprised Benjamin when Geraldine Slater and Byron Hill asked him to help them start an Indian club.

"How come?" Benjamin said.

"How come what?"

"How come all of a sudden you want an *Indian* club?"

"I had an Indian grandmother," Byron said with a grin.

Benjamin saw Geraldine glance uneasily at Byron. It must be her idea, he thought. It wouldn't be Byron's. Byron's father ran one of the charter-boat businesses working out of Salt Chuck. Salmon fishing filled the boats with tourists every summer. But no Indians were ever hired to help with the charters. Not by Byron's father.

"Mr. Kerry said he'd be the sponsor. He likes all that Indian stuff."

It was the same as saying, "*I* don't like that Indian stuff," thought Benjamin.

"I think it's a wonderful idea," Geraldine said.

"Mr. Kerry knows all about Indian art," said Byron. "He says we could make our own designs for baskets and make a float for the Fourth of July parade. Or maybe make our own totem pole." Byron grinned. "You know, I've never been top man on a totem pole. Har — har — har."

The sound plopped in front of them like balloons filled with water.

Benjamin said, "Indian culture to you non-Indians always means only canoes and baskets and totem poles. But to Indians it is much more. It was their way of life. It was the way they coped with nature. It was what nature meant to them."

Geraldine looked for a moment as if she had sucked a lemon. She blinked her eyes rapidly and smiled weakly. Uncertainly. But Byron wasn't really listening.

"Maybe what we could do is require everyone to take an Indian name for the club meetings. Like Crazy Horse or Sixkiller. Wow — that one's for me! Our insignia could be a red feather or something like that. Man! This is going to be fun! We'll call our meetings Powwows!"

Benjamin turned away, opened the door of his car, and slid in.

"Hey man! Where you going?"

"He doesn't like the idea," Geraldine said. She was

standing hunched over, hugging her books against her chest. There were raspberry blotches on her face and her eyes were beginning to water. "And you know what," she said. "I don't either much. It's a dumb idea. Even if Mr. Haley thinks it's great."

An Indian club for Indians *and* whites. That made it nondiscriminatory! Benjamin laughed.

"It *was* a great idea," Benjamin said. He flipped on the ignition. Put his car in reverse, slammed his foot on the pedal. He backed out with a squeal and went hurtling down the street. As if he were chasing the thunderbird.

He heard Byron yelling after him. "YOU CRAZY INDIAN!"

12

Open House Held

Approximately forty-four people attended the open house held in the lovely double-wide mobile home of Mr. and Mrs. Ray Holt of Salt Chuck.

A delicious baked-salmon dinner complete with all the trimmings was served. The salmon was baked by Mrs. Warren Holt, Sr.

After dinner, numbers were drawn and those with lucky numbers taped under their plates were the delighted recipients of hand-woven baskets made by Mrs. Warren Holt, Sr.

Mrs. Ray Holt presented gifts to all present, then opened the open-house gifts. She thanked all for attending.

Assisting with preparations for the open house were Mr. and Mrs. Warren Holt, Sr.

13

I Hate You

I GET A WATCH when I graduate," Louise said. "My father said he'd give me one. For a graduation gift. He said it would be worth celebrating. If I graduate." She made a face as she pushed her fist into the sand of the beach. Her father didn't think she'd ever graduate.

"I'm supposed to celebrate my graduation by giving a gift. That's what Indians do. Giving things away is a big thing in Indian culture," Benjamin said. "Last year an old Indian woman sold off a piece of her land in Salt Chuck and she gave a big dinner and gifts to everybody in the village. It was a real old potlatch. She gave everything she got away."

"My mother would think she was potted."

"She was just being an Indian. The more you give away, the more status you have if you're an Indian."

"The more you have the better you are, if you're white," Louise told him.

"That's what was so confusing to me. For a long time. When I was little. An Indian kid grows up in a white man's world and he is told to look up to the people who have the most. A big car. A fine house. Lots of money in the bank. That means you are somebody."

"Well, you are, aren't you? If you're smart enough to have all that."

"Indians don't believe that."

"My mother thinks the more things she has, the more she is. Our neighbor had a party last night — to show off her new rug. Wow! She really acted like she thought she was somebody."

"When my mother gives a party in Douglas, she still gives everybody gifts. Little ones, anyway."

"That's really nice."

"I guess you can't stop doing things that are part of you. Not altogether."

They stared at the rolling waves.

"I like the ocean," Benjamin said. "The wind socks. The waves slap back. One two — one two."

Louise laughed. "You're mad as the ocean! It's foaming at the mouth." She moved her feet away from the spume.

"A long time ago, the Indians here were whalers. Right here in Salt Chuck. They were seal hunters too." He licked the salt off his lips with his tongue. Louise dug a hole in the sand. "That's what's so great about that ancient village found up the coast. They were whalers too. Maybe part of this same tribe. They hunted in long dugout canoes. With harpoons."

"What do you think happened to the village?"

"Leo said it was something like Pompeii. You know. Lava flowing down. Covering everything. Sealing it off. Only instead of lava, this was mud. Because of the rain. The village was right on the edge of the shore. A hill behind it. One day the whole hill just slid down and covered the village. Just like that. One moment a village full of people. And the next — nothing."

Louise shuddered.

"That's the way Leo thinks it happened. The mud all dried into clay finally. It sealed everything up. Everything under it was preserved. Today it is exactly as it was hundreds of years ago."

Louise listened to the boom of the waves. The screaming of the gulls.

"Sometimes I think I hear the sound of whales," Benjamin said.

"What do they sound like?"

"They sing," he said. "A kind of song."

"You mean a song like birds?"

"A different kind of tune. It goes up and down like mountaintops. High for a while and then low. It's a whole song but it has no beginning and no end."

"Ah, you haven't really heard them!"

"I didn't say I really heard them. I said I *thought* I heard them."

She stared out at the rolling gray undersides of the white waves. Whales' stomachs. She tried to think of Salt Chuck as a whalers' village. The only sign of it she could see was a kind of whale totem standing in front of the tourist motel. She had heard that the Indians believed that the wolves left the forest and entered the sea where they became killer whales. Louise wondered how they could really believe that. She shivered.

"I'm going to die in the ocean," Benjamin said. "When I die."

"Hey!" She jumped up. "Come on. I'm freezing here."

He lunged after her.

"You can't run, Indian!" she shouted, and he made a flying tackle. She felt herself grasped by the hips and flung onto the soft sand of the beach. He held her there, pressing down on top of her.

"Ptooey," she said, pushing away his salty lips. "Let me up."

They had to climb over the pile of driftwood logs to get back to the car.

They drove up the dirt road to Salt Chuck. Along the village street. Past the Community Center. To the slight rise where the Coast Guard station house was. He parked the car facing the ocean. They sat there together, silently, looking out at a rock. It pushed up out of the sea almost two hundred feet high. An island.

"When I was a kid," said Benjamin, "any Indian who couldn't swim out to that rock and back was called a *hoquat*. That means *white man*."

It seemed to Louise a long way to swim. The rock looked cold and gray. A few needle-branched trees stuck up out of the top, bent and sparse. She listened to the noise of the crashing waves beating against the cold sleek sides of the island and she wound her arms around herself in the need suddenly to feel warm.

"Once I climbed to the top," he said.

"Way up there?"

"That's what they used to call it. Ah-Kah-Lahkt or Sech-Hoh-Lahkt. It meant *way up there*."

"Looks steep."

'There's a trail. You can't see it anymore. Nobody goes up there now. It zig-zags. Very steep and very narrow. You have to go single file."

She started out. There was what appeared to be a flat place on top.

"Once about two hundred years ago — that's what my mother said — the village was raided by a neighboring tribe. They carried off the chief's daughter. So the Salt Chuck men went after her in their 40-foot whaling canoes. They got there at midnight and set fire to a big storehouse, found the girl and brought her back. Then

everyone in Salt Chuck climbed the trail to the top of
the rock. They carried stones with them. When the
raiders came back and tried to climb up after them, the
stones were hurled down on their heads. Another time
the villagers heated water up there and dumped it down
on the heads of the attackers coming up."

Benjamin grinned. "You'd never believe it but Salt
Chuck once had the fiercest warriors on the coast."

Louise glanced back at the seedy village. "You're
right," she said. "I don't believe it."

"It was a lot different then," Benjamin said. "They
had pride in their own culture. And in themselves.
They caught fish and harpooned whales and seals in the
sea. They dug the razor clams on the beach. They found
deer, elk, wild berries, roots and other food in the forest.
They spoke their own language. And had their own religion. No one told them what to do. This was their
country. They were free men."

"Before the settlers came," Louise said. Then she
wished she hadn't.

His smile drew tight. Taut. Like a rope stretched
across a road. Or a rubber band pulled out ready to
snap.

"Right." His voice stretched hard too. "That was
before the white man came."

They sat there for a while just watching the ocean.

Benjamin opened a can of beer, tasted it, and wiped
his lips. "Want some?"

She took a swallow, then shook her head. He set it on the dashboard.

"I like you," he said, "but I hate you too."

She looked at the can of beer. *Indians can't drink.* That's what everyone said.

She laughed. The sound came out, unexpectedly and a little hoarsely.

He took another swallow and tossed the can out the window. "You think I'm crazy?"

"No," she said solemnly. "I don't think you're crazy."

He slid back and rested his head on the seat back.

"Sometimes I hate all whites," he said. "Do you know that? I hate them for pushing the Indians onto the reservations. I hate them for always acting like they're better than" — there was only the slightest pause — "us."

Louise moved sideways, pressing her back against the car door. She looked at his face. An Indian face. Smooth. A calm sea. A river stone. It was a strong face. A shadow passed over it. Like a door closing. Closed tight. With the key thrown away.

He turned toward her suddenly, reaching out. His hands grabbed her shoulders. His fingers pressed tightly. Close to her neck. Too tightly.

"Sometimes," he said, not at all calmly, "I hate you!"

She couldn't shriek. She could hardly breathe.

He pulled his hands away from her neck.

They drove silently homeward.

14

The Ring

THE NEXT DAY she lost his ring. She didn't know how she lost it. She looked down at her hand — and it was not there.

Her skin prickled. A fearful feeling. To Benjamin giving her his ring was like giving her part of himself. And she had lost it.

"What's the matter?" said her mother.

"Nothing."

"You look like you'd seen a ghost." Her mother yawned. "Y'know, sometimes I wonder why we ever came to this town. Crazy things happen here. I've never been in a town like this. Maybe it's because of the Indians."

Louise didn't feel like arguing with her mother about Indians. "Did you see my ring?" she asked.

"What ring?"

"The ring Benjamin gave me. It was flat and gold and had a little blue insignia on it. It said seventy-one."

"Louise, I've been meaning to talk to you about that."

"About what?"

Her mother was a pretty woman, thought Louise, until she put on that expression. It made deep furrows down the side of her cheeks. It made her look like she'd forgotten to put in her false teeth.

"Well, I don't like what I'm hearing about that Benjamin Turner."

Louise paused in her search of the silverware drawer. It might have slipped off her finger, she thought, when she was putting away the dishes. There were a million places it could be. The thought of losing it was really making her shake.

She straightened her shoulders and stood up, looking her mother straight in the eyes. "What did you hear?"

"If you want to know," her mother said sharply, "he's stirring those Indian kids up all over school."

It was so ridiculous that Louise laughed. "Where'd you hear that?"

Her mother raised her eyebrows coyly. "I heard it. You don't have to believe me, but I heard it."

Louise took her handbag off the chair and dumped its contents out over the kitchen table. She scattered the things about, looking for the ring. "Yeah," she said, "just like you heard that Leslie Enson took an overdose of heroin and was dead. Funny about that, because just this morning I saw Leslie and Betty Lee walking down Main Street. Leslie didn't look very *dead* to me."

"What are you looking for?" her mother said sharply.

"My ring."

"What ring?"

"Oh for heaven's sake, Mother. You never listen."

Her own words set up an odd echo. "He never listens," Benjamin had told her bitterly when he came out of the principal's office. "Haley never listens to Indians."

She went over to Leo's to look for her ring. She looked all over the big overstuffed chair where she had sat with Benjamin, and under the creaky couch, and in the kitchen through the records on the cupboard shelves.

"What's so important about a little ring?" said Leo. "Was it ruby? Diamond? Pearl?"

She shook her head. "It was Benjamin's."

She felt Leo's full attention and turned slowly around to meet his eyes.

"I'm afraid he'll be mad," she said. "I mean — I'm really afraid — "

He smiled amiably. "Benjamin's a good guy."

"I know. But" — her smile felt shaky — "you see, I'm no Indian."

Leo picked up the big pot off the stove, swilled it around a bit, and poured two mugs of coffee. He set them down on the table. They sipped at the drinks, each of them, for a moment. "It's only lukewarm," said Leo.

"It's lovely."

"Benjamin. He's something else again," said Leo.

"I know."

"Beautiful."

"I know."

"We talk," he said. "He comes here and we sit up half the night sometimes. Just talking."

"Mr. Otis calls it rapping."

Leo took another sip of his lukewarm coffee. He hunched toward her, his arms all over the table. "I don't think he's ever talked to anyone else like he's talked to me. Except maybe his brother. The one who died."

"I guess we don't talk that much," Louise said.

"Sometimes I *feel* as if I were his brother." Leo held up two fingers pressed closely together. "I feel that close."

Louise nodded.

"It's funny, you know. Because I'm not at all like his brother. I'm not as close to his age. And I'm not even an Indian. But somehow we are, we really are, brothers."

Louise swallowed too big a mouthful, coughed, and choked a little. Leo reached over and gave a firm swat to her back.

"I'm all right." She wiped her eyes.

He went on talking. "Ever see a cocoon change into a butterfly? Or a tadpole into a frog? What happens seems a kind of magic. Like a frog becoming a prince. Witchcraft. But it's not. It's perfectly natural. A metamorphosis. That's what is happening to Benjamin now."

Her mind boggled a little. "A prince?"

"An Indian," Leo said.

"Oh."

"It isn't quite over yet," said Leo.

"What?"

"The metamorphosis. Benjamin has been like fighting two worlds. Right now he's not in either exactly."

"Oh," she said again. She finished the lukewarm coffee. She stared thoughtfully at the bushy fringe on Leo's upper lip. "You know what? I went out with him last night."

"Yes."

"I think the metamorphosis is over."

He looked thoughtfully back at her. "You could be right."

"I'm right," she said. And she knew she had lost more than the ring.

15

Dig Trip

THE TELEPHONE rang in the principal's office. It rang sharply, demandingly, too early in the day, thought Mr. Haley, to portend any good.

He let it ring two more times before picking it up. "Hello!" he said firmly. He gave a lift to his voice. A lift he did not feel.

He hadn't slept at all well. He was tired. He hadn't even looked into Mr. Otis' window as he had come into the building. He was a little late this morning, an unusual thing for him. No one was in the outer office and school had begun.

Only a few days before he had heard about a planned trip to the archeological dig out there on the Cape. Benjamin Turner had been at the bottom of that. Principal Haley had met the Indian bus and asked them not to go.

He had told them he would arrange to select an official school day and a school bus would take them and the proper chaperone. They would have to have the proper signed permission excuses from their parents, of course. They had not brought any.

But Friday there was no school — a teacher's conference day — nor was there any on Saturday or Sunday, of course. Monday and Tuesday he had been busy with other things, and this was Wednesday. He saw the date on the desk calendar. March 24, 1971.

The voice over the telephone was the custodian's. "Thought you'd want to know. There are some Indian kids outside your school. And they're leaving. They said they got signed excuses to leave."

Mr. Haley looked down at his desk. In a neat pile, placed there by someone, was a bunch of folded slips.

"Hold them!" he commanded. "Tell them I have not yet authorized any such trip."

"They said they're going!"

"It will mean truancy if they leave," said Haley. "I'm coming right out there."

He hurried down the hall out to the parking lot.

A group of Indian students were clustered there around Benjamin's car and one other. Mostly all juniors.

"Hey! Here comes Haley," he heard one shout. Not even a Mr., just Haley.

He bore down on them, walking rapidly, his chin held high.

"What's going on here?" he demanded.

Benjamin grinned at him, politely. "Everybody brought their permission excuses, just like you said. We're going to the dig."

Mr. Haley had the momentary feeling that the small group surged toward him. He stepped back, hastily. Then he realized it had only been a wave of his own apprehension. He held himself firmly erect. "I must tell you," he said, "that if you leave without my authorization, you, every one of you, will be suspended from school." He turned about to leave, hesitated, and turned to speak directly to Benjamin. "I warn you, Benjamin, an action of this kind guarantees extreme disciplinary measures." He turned then and walked back into the school. He had given him fair warning, he told himself.

All in all he had given Benjamin Turner more than a full share of attention, the principal reassured himself as he reentered his office. He had listened to Benjamin innumerable times; he had tried to help him. He had even taken time to talk with the boy when other matters had demanded his concentration.

On the other hand, Benjamin had continually demonstrated his uncooperativeness. That audio-visual project, for instance. Now why hadn't he gone ahead with that? Then, for some reason, Mr. Haley recalled the time he and another teacher had found Benjamin and a white student in the center of the school grounds — drunk.

Benjamin at the wheel of his father's car. Still, Mr. Haley reminded himself, he had tried to protect him. He had simply reached in and removed the car keys. Leaving the boys sitting in the car, the principal had walked off, taking the keys with him. The next day, Benjamin's father had thanked the principal for the action.

Mr. Haley sat down at his desk.

He made a check of all the Indian students. Eleven were absent without permission. Eleven including Benjamin Turner. Principal Haley sat there a few moments. He remembered suddenly how he had felt aiming at the eyes of the buck. A shotgun in his hand. An odd memory at this moment, he thought. Totally irrelevant.

The telephone rang.

"This is Mrs. Ida Homan. Is my grandchild in school?" An Indian parent. Though most of them didn't seem to care whether their kids were in school or not. The name was on his list of eleven.

"He is not in school," the principal said firmly. "He is not in school and I think you should know that he has been warned that he will be suspended."

"You can't do that," the woman said, getting excited. "You suspend my grandson and that's the end of school for him. He'll never go back."

"That's not my concern," Principal Haley said as politely as possible. "I can't go chasing after him."

"Maybe you can't," she said. "But the sheriff can.

You call him and get those kids back to school."

Principal Haley replaced the telephone. It was as if a trigger had been pulled, he reflected. And it was too late to change the aim.

16

Bugle Call

WE HAVE an old Indian maxim," Mr. Turner said to the principal. "Before judging a man, walk three moons in his moccasins."

Benjamin sat in the principal's office between his father and his mother. He stared at the fake inkwell on the principal's desk. Inside his head, a song was singing.

> I wanna be an Indian
> I wanna be red
> I wanna be free
> Or I wanna be dead.

It went rapping along so solidly inside that he wondered if the principal could hear it too. But the principal didn't seem to be hearing what was going on in Benjamin's head. No more clearly, anyway, than he was hearing what Benjamin's father said.

His father talked like an old Indian chief. He looked like a chief. Maybe because he was standing up. Even his face was quiet like an Indian.

The principal said, "As far as I am concerned, Benjamin had been warned. He has broken the rules, thus being truant."

> *I wanna be an Indian*
> *I wanna be red*
> *I wanna be free*
> *Or I wanna be dead.*

It was an Indian "My country 'tis of thee" thought Benjamin. Like a national anthem. But it was also a bugle call. And a pledge of allegiance.

It had been singing along inside his head ever since they had left the school grounds yesterday morning. It had pounded along with him through the one hour and forty-five minute drive to the Cape. It hadn't stopped. Not once. Not even when the marshal's car was there waiting for them.

They didn't even get to take the old Indian trail out to the ocean where the dig was. They didn't even get to pile out of the car to stretch. They had to sit tight and go right back. But the song kept on going.

They were all brought back to Douglas. But instead of taking them back to school, they were hauled off to the marshal's office. Benjamin had to stay there for a while. The other kids were sent back to school.

He hadn't missed anything at school that day. Harold came by to tell him. Except Mr. Otis' calendar. Mr. Haley saw it. He took it back to his office with him. But not before Harold had copied some of it off. He showed it to Benjamin.

The white calendar squares had been impartially designated with appropriate holidays. March 7 was Sex Day. March 13, Drunk Day. March 17, Booze Donation Day. March 24, the date of the unscheduled trip to the Indian dig was named Dictator Haley Day. Looking ahead to the next month was B.S. Day. Smoking Pot Day. St. Otis Day. St. Screw Day. St. Pregnant Day. Four Letter Word Day. The last day in the month was highlighted as Kill a Principal Day.

It was nice of Harold.

Benjamin listened to his song again.

> *I wanna be an Indian*
> *I wanna be red*
> *I wanna be free*
> *Or I wanna be dead.*

He listened to the principal too.

"I told Benjamin he would be suspended if he left. So he was warned."

He listened to his father.

"Benjamin was trying to help Indians in this school. You say yourself, the school dropout rate for Indians is twice the national average. Almost 90 percent is a lot. Perhaps you judge Benjamin too hastily. That is why I ask — walk three moons." He sat down.

Principal Haley cleared his throat. "That's all very good, Mr. Turner, but your son has broken school rules. Disciplinary action is indicated."

"White man's rules," said Benjamin's mother suddenly. It was the first time she had spoken.

"We have only one set of rules here, Mrs. Turner," Mr. Haley said sharply.

Benjamin knew his mother was a little hard of hearing. She was shy about it. He had never heard her speak up outside of the Indian community like this before. He looked at her in surprise.

"My Benjamin must go to school," she said. "He has four brothers older. All went to school here in Douglas for a few years. All dropped out. Benjamin is not like his brothers. He likes to study. He makes A's, maybe some B's. Mostly A's. He will be a big man someday. Our Indians need a big man like my son Benjamin."

Mr. Haley glanced politely at the watch on his wrist. But Mrs. Turner was not yet finished.

"We are a small people, we Indians at Salt Chuck. Our village on the ocean, it is only a tiny place. In my great-grandfather's day, our lands stretched nine hundred square miles." She swept her arms widely across his desk,

taking in all the town of Douglas. "Our territory today covers about five hundred ninety-five acres." She
gazed significantly at Mr. Haley but he did not seem to
be impressed.

"That adds up to not quite one square mile," Benjamin said. Without interrupting the sound in his head.

Mr. Haley cleared his throat again, and said stiffly, "I
have no quarrel with Benjamin's ability, Mrs. Turner.
But rules are rules. The same for a white student as for
an Indian student."

"You treat Indian students no different than white?"
Benjamin's mother asked clearly.

"No different," Mr. Haley said.

"Hah!" said Mrs. Turner.

Mr. Haley stared at the papers on his desk. The
silence beat down on them loud as a drum.

"Your son, Mrs. Turner, was suspended because he
used the wrong procedure in attempting to make a field
trip with students during school hours. The trip which
was taken was not properly sponsored."

Then the principal stood up. He looked down upon
them from behind his desk. He said formally, "Benjamin, you are suspended indefinitely pending an official
school board meeting which will be held" — he paused
to consult his desk calendar — "on April 22."

Benjamin's father stood up. Politely he nodded.
And Benjamin and the song and his parents silently filed
out.

17

Notice

To: Mr. Lloyd Otis

This is to notify you that you are hereby suspended from your teaching duties until the next scheduled meeting of the Board of Directors' of the Douglas School District No..201. Said meeting will be held in the library of the Douglas High School at 8:00 p.m., April 22, 1971.

Your suspension is based upon inadequate performance of your teaching duties, non-compliance with directives as presented by the administration, and the presence of non-professional material in your room. We shall request your immediate dismissal at the above mentioned meeting.

Sincerely,yours,
Gregory E. Haley
HIGH SCHOOL PRINCIPAL
Richard Stevenson
SUPERINTENDENT

18

Teacher Notice

School Board Meeting

Teachers may want to attend
the regular school board meeting
this Thursday evening, April 22,
to be held in the high school library.
There will probably be a good
representation from Salt Chuck.

19

Walk Three Moons

LOUISE's mother didn't want her to go to the meeting. "I don't see why you even want to go."

"We're still friends. Even if we're not going around together anymore."

Her mother was glad they had broken up, even though she said she was sorry.

"They won't really expel him," Louise told her mother. "They didn't expel that George Heck or Johnny Hony. And they made a lot more trouble at school than Benjamin Turner ever did."

"Six of one and half a dozen of another are the same to you but maybe not to the school board," her mother said in that way she had sometimes. Like a warning.

But it wasn't until Louise pushed her way into the crowded library where the meeting was going on that she thought of what her mother meant. Those boys that made trouble weren't Indians.

When Louise looked at Benjamin, she knew at once why she had really wanted to come. He saw her. And his smile turned on like a light on a dark porch. She noticed how much he had let his hair grow. It hung way over his eyes in front and went down the back of his neck. He really looked like an Indian.

Louise waved and moved toward the back of the room. Where the Indians were, most of them. She stood against the back wall with them for a while. Then she saw an empty chair, and made her way to it. She sat right behind Mr. Otis.

It took a while for everyone to get settled. Louise listening to the talking. Like fat bees buzzing. And the coughs. Engines backfiring. She smelled the dry book smell.

No one much was smiling. Except Mr. Otis. This was all "bunko" to him.

The four members of the school board and Principal Haley and the superintendent droned on about a lot of other things first. No one paid much attention. No one really listened closely until Principal Haley recommended the expulsion of Benjamin Turner from Douglas High School. His voice sounded no different than it did when he was talking about the carpet or the school bus.

He reviewed it all methodically from the paper in his hand. He called it "disruptive school behavior" and quoted state laws regarding pupil attendance. He read off the rules in regard to motor vehicles on the school grounds and the laws listing cause for suspension and/or expulsion from school. It all seemed very cut and dried. Like packaged noodles. It was hard for Louise to even relate it to Benjamin.

When the principal stopped reading off his Rules and Laws, everyone turned to look at Benjamin. They waited expectantly. He didn't even stand up. He sat there staring at a couple of books he had brought with him. Louise could see the titles on the end covers. *Crazy Horse* by Shannon Garst. And *Custer Died for Your Sins* by Vine Deloria, Jr. They weren't school library books. She wondered why he had brought books to the meeting.

"Well, Benjamin?" the superintendent prodded.

Benjamin pushed himself up straight. "I know a lot of you look on me as a radical, no-good, long-haired hippie."

Louise heard some of her classmates snicker. She saw the adults in the audience begin to frown.

"Well, I'm not," said Benjamin. "I don't think of myself as a militant. That's a word created by whites. Indians have been here thirty thousand years and now whites force us to live according to another culture. Indians have a right to preserve their own culture. And their pride. I've never seen a militant Indian."

The superintendent said, "We haven't got all night,

Benjamin. Let's stick to the subject. Which is" — he referred to the agenda sheet in front of him — "the consideration of your expulsion. Do you have anything to say in regard to that?"

"It used to be if an Indian was kicked out of school, he would go back to the reservation and brag about it," Benjamin said loudly. "But now that's changing. Indian youth are demanding to go back to school. My purpose is to make other people aware it's changing. That's what I'm trying to do." He turned to the principal. "That's what I was trying to do when I asked you not once, but many different times, for permission to form an Indian Culture Club. You said no."

"I said then, and I will say it again now," said Principal Haley, a little testily, "that the school will not allow any group that excludes others, because this is discrimination itself. No Indian group in the school can exclude whites. Nor can any white group exclude Indians."

"But you whites do exclude Indians," someone shouted from the audience. "Sure we can join a school club. No law against it. But if we do we have to sit in the back of the room. Or everybody in the club shuns us completely."

There were more mutterings and murmurings. The superintendent banged the gavel. One of the board members said loudly that such remarks concerning discrimination in the school were completely "off base."

An Indian laughed.

"Civil rights is not an issue tonight," another member of the board remarked firmly.

"What is then?" Mr. Otis challenged.

An Indian in the back of the room stood up and began to talk loudly. "I was kicked out of school and I never graduated. So I know what I'm talking about. You don't care whether Indians graduate or not. You never cared and you never will. And that's all I've got to say."

The white faces began to look angry too.

A young Indian woman rose. "I went to school here, and I didn't graduate either. But I wasn't kicked out. I just left. My brother didn't graduate either. He was kicked out. Do you think that makes any difference? You don't look for any answers to the problems. You just get rid of them. That's how you solve them. That's what you're doing now!" She sat down shaking.

The school board members passed glances between them. There was a little clearing of throats. And discreet coughs behind hands. And some shuffling of feet under the long table. The superintendent stopped the rumblings of talk with his gavel. "Well, let's get on with it," he said.

"A person makes of himself what he wants to be," a board member said pointedly.

Nothing anybody had said so far had made any difference, thought Louise. It was just as if they had made up their minds to expel Benjamin before they even got there.

"Stands to reason — if a club for Indian students only was formed, then there should also be a club open only for white students. And everybody knows *that's* discrimination."

Benjamin's father stood up. He went up to the front of the room to talk. He talked slowly as if he were making a speech. He said things that made the board members frown. But he said them.

"Discrimination exists here in the high school whether you believe it or not. I don't like to be told to go back to the reservation where I belong. This is racism and ninety percent of the Indian children from Salt Chuck have this problem."

Then a lady jumped up. "Discrimination?" she said. "I can tell you there's no discrimination in Douglas. Why I've lived here in Douglas all my life — and I've never seen any of this so-called discrimination." She sat down amidst a smattering of clapping.

One Indian woman who lived in Douglas spoke up for Benjamin. She talked of the aims of the culture club he had tried to form. How he wanted to give the Indian children in the school pride in themselves. How much they needed that pride. And how much they needed to express themselves as individuals.

Louise looked at the faces of the board members. She might as well have been talking to a cement wall, thought Louise. That was her mother's favorite expression. "Talk to you; talk to a wall." It fitted here anyway.

Another Indian woman said loudly, "Benjamin Turner was trying to help the young ones. There was discrimination all over but the faculty didn't see it. The kids go through the halls with their heads lowered. That's the real problem!"

"You have a solution," someone called out from near the back of the room.

"What's *he* opening his big mouth for?" someone muttered. And someone else said, "He's an outsider, why should he talk?"

The man sitting next to Louise tapped Mr. Otis on the shoulder. "You paying him?" he said with a wink, and he snickered.

But Mr. Otis looked just as surprised as everybody else. But pleased. You could see he was sort of pleased.

The speaker stood up and introduced himself. He raised his voice over all the shufflings. "The solution originated in the minds of the Indian students in this school," he said clearly. "They have been trying to implement their solution for the past year and have been unsuccessful because of the lack of cooperation, understanding, and sincerity of the school's administration."

"You have no right to speak," a woman called out. But he went right on.

"Because the students felt so strongly about their problems and their solution, they defied the administration. The result being the suspension of their spokesman."

"That's just your opinion!" a burly citizen called out.

The superintendent frowned.

"The Indian students have proposed that they be allowed to meet like any other club, to overcome their shared problems. To develop as a group a better self-image, study their cultural heritage, remove the stereotype that non-Indian teachers and students have of Indians, encourage attendance and performance as a group, participate in school activities as a club to make school more enjoyable for them, and to communicate problems and recommendations to teachers and the administration."

"Sitdown," someone hollered.

"The whole concept is so positive that I cannot see why it was turned down. Yet the administration feels that to set up such a club would be discriminatory against non-Indians! This must be a joke!" And he sat down.

The school board members listened politely. Just like they had listened to everybody. Their expressions were stuck to their faces like paper on a wall. But they voted to expel Benjamin. Unanimously. They thought they were being fair, Louise decided. They really thought they were being entirely fair.

Then they read the charges against Mr. Otis, the biology teacher. Ten points regarding his classroom and his teaching procedures were read off. Like a manifesto. The board decided that none of the ten points had been improved on and asked Mr. Otis if he had something to say about it too. He said loudly, "These charges are just a lot of bunk. You think I'm guilty because of what I believe and what I feel. If you didn't fire me, I would resign anyway. I can no longer continue in a teaching job when I do not feel my heart is in it."

His immediate release was then voted on. He was fired.

Louise walked slowly down the hall. Behind her came a little huddle of schoolgirls.

"Well, I say there's no discrimination here," one said. "Mrs. Phenny was right. I've lived here all my life too and I've never seen any."

"I've never discriminated against anyone in my whole life."

"It's probably nothing but their imagination. Indians act real funny about some things."

"You can't really depend on what they say anyway. They don't have any responsibility. They're always getting drunk."

"Anyway," said the first girl. "I think Benjamin Turner deserved getting kicked out. That's what my father said. And that's what I say, too."

Louise stopped, and they divided and pushed right past her. They didn't even notice who she was. Or if they did, they didn't even care that she had heard. Now I know what it feels like to be an Indian, she thought. And moved along behind them.

"I never did like that Mr. Otis. I'm glad he's not coming back."

"I never learned anything about biology in his class."

Another added more emphatically, "I never learned anything at all!"

Louise hung around a little. Waiting until Benjamin came out. She would tell him that she wanted to be his girl again. That it made no difference to her that he was expelled.

He came finally, walking slowly. But his head wasn't hanging down.

"Benjamin?"

He stopped and regarded her slowly in that Indian way. An Indian takes his time making up his mind about people, Louise reflected. He always reserves judgment until their actions show what kind of people they really are. It pleased her to have been able to recognize and appreciate that. As if she were getting to be a little bit Indian too.

He smiled at her. "How do you feel?" she said gently.

He shook his hair off his face. "Wow!" he said. They began to walk down the hallway together. "There were a lot of beautiful people in there tonight. A lot of them!"

Beautiful? She thought of the room full of righteous expressions on indignant white faces. The ugly frowns of some of them. The blankly unsympathetic eyes.

"They came all the way from Salt Chuck to support me," Benjamin said. "They turned out just for me. Did you hear them? Wasn't that beautiful?"

Louise felt the sudden gush of tears in her eyes before she even knew she was crying.

"I'll never understand you, Benjamin. I'll never understand you as long as I live!"

20

They

WELL, that takes care of that problem." Geraldine Slater's father turned the car into their driveway.

Geraldine waited for the next words. They came, just as she had expected they would.

Her mother said, "Poor devil."

"I can't say I feel sorry for him," Geraldine heard a woman say in the Pay 'n Save the next day. "I am certain that the school would not have objected if the kids had been properly escorted by responsible adults."

"Of course not!"

Geraldine left the store.

"And why such a trip on a school day anywhere when there are holidays and weekends?" Mrs. Balstrade came out of the bank.

Geraldine passed the tavern.

"We'd certainly expect our school board to react if a group of white youngsters were to take off for an un-authorized trip led by irresponsible types."

"That's what I say. When dealing with school chil-dren, the school board just has to stand by the standards set by the most strict of parents. It's their duty."

Geraldine went into the drugstore. She picked up a jar of Mum and waited for the pharmacist to wait on her. He was busy talking to a shaving cream customer.

"Well, you know what I feel? I feel sorry for them — those people who stood up for Benjamin Turner. It doesn't make any difference in the long run whether he was right or wrong in what he did. I just feel sorry for them."

"Sorry!" It was an explosion. "What do you mean, sorry?"

"Because you know and I know — it wasn't Benjamin Turner's idea in the first place. All that talk about his people and their pride and their dignity!" He snorted.

Geraldine put the Mum back on the shelf and went out. She walked past the Sears store and the variety store and the dress shop.

"Take it from me — he was used! I'm not mention-ing any names. But you know who I mean."

"They came into town stirring up the Indians, talking about 'identity.'"

"They put words in his mouth, set him up as a pigeon . . ."

"We never had any trouble with the Indians before they hit Douglas. Now tell me. Did we ever have any trouble with Indians?"

"I'm looking at it with an open mind. And they sure primed him."

"Well, you can't condemn him, not completely. Just look at the newspaper any day. Young people all over the country being exploited in this same manner."

Geraldine crossed the street.

"I tell you I feel sorry for those Indians. Because that's how it was and anybody with a brain in his head could see it."

"They say it's the school's fault that Indians are not succeeding. But the truth is it's the fault of the Indians themselves."

"Well, I know one thing for sure. The school has done everything that could be expected to teach them to act like white students."

"Lazy ignorant bastards. Getting up there and complaining about discrimination."

Geraldine hastened along. The words came right after her —

"Hell, they can't even spell the word right!"

Geraldine stopped hurrying. She had this funny feeling. As if she had come all the way around again to where she had started. She stopped right where she was and looked down.

Something gleamed at her from the sidewalk. A bit of gold. She picked it up. It was somebody's ring. A class ring. It said '71 on it. Just like Harold's. She stuck it on her finger and went home.

21

Hamburger Special

Louise didn't see the fight Benjamin got into in front of the café. She didn't ask him about it and he didn't come around to tell her. They weren't seeing each other much at all. Not even as friends. People kept asking her about the fight. As if she should know. And she didn't.

But she was sure she knew just how it happened. She could see the whole thing as it must have been.

Benjamin sitting on the café stool. Squinting up at the menu on the wall. Studying it carefully. And then deciding to order what he always ordered.

She saw Lila the waitress filling coffee cups. Slopping over onto the saucers. Too busy to care much.

"A hamburger special," Benjamin said.

Lila went right on filling the cups. He thought she didn't hear him. When she came by again, he said it a little louder.

Lila didn't hear him that time either. She went to the back of the counter, wet a cloth, wrung it out slowly and started to wipe the counter.

Another logger came in. The street was always full of logging trucks.

"Coffee?" Lila sang out.

"Black," he said. "And hot." He saw Benjamin and took a seat next to him.

"A hamburger special," Benjamin said again. The other eaters began to smirk.

"What's on the menu for a real Indian, Lila?" the man prodded helpfully. "Now none of that horrible white man stuff. You've got to give him real Indian food."

"Like what?" she said. Encouraging him. Egging him on.

"Like maybe sun-dried smelt, well walked over. And spotted up by crows and gulls. Maybe a little whale bacon on the side gathered from overripe whale and smoked in the rafters of the long house. Pretty delectable!" He smacked his lips with a loud sucking noise and enjoyed the laughing.

Benjamin sat looking at the unwiped counter before him.

"How about offering up a little bobcat stew? Maybe

a few stink eggs of salmon. Now that would be a fitting
cultural Indian meal."

Benjamin slid off the stool and went outside.

An Indian sat on the curb out there. Maybe he had
come in from Salt Chuck for a bottle of whiskey. Maybe
he had just been having a little beer.

The logger came out right behind Benjamin and saw
him there. "Move!" he ordered. "Don't you know you're
dirtying up the streets this way?"

The Indian said, "I'm sorry."

"Well, move!" the man said. He was mean about
it.

The Indian moved, muttered, and stepped up on the
curb unsteadily.

Benjamin sat down on the curb in his place.

The fellow took Benjamin by the elbow and jerked
him up onto his feet again. "You heard me, Injun. We
don't want any dirty troublemakers around here."

Benjamin pulled away from him. "That's not the
problem," he said.

"Well, and what is the problem?" And he smiled at
his buddy coming out of the café.

"The problem is my people walk around with their
heads hanging down. They're even ashamed to talk to
each other. Because what we haven't got anymore is
our pride."

"Pride!?" The second man spit it out as if it had been
a worm.

"Indians have a right to preserve their culture and their pride," Benjamin said.

"Now I know a little about this here pride, myself. The reason you Injuns got no pride is because you don't have any to git. Hell, I wouldn't hire an Indian to work for me if he paid me. They get drunker than a skunk. They don't try, they show no initiative, and when the chips are down they don't assert themselves. Pride!" He gave a loud laugh.

Benjamin ducked his head and barreled into the man's stomach. The fellow slammed back at him. It didn't take him long to flip Benjamin to the sidewalk. His buddy helped to slap Benjamin around a bit. Somebody in the café called the marshal. But it took twenty minutes for his deputy to make his way out of the office only a block and a half away and get down there.

The old Indian shouted, "They beat him up. Two of them. They jumped on him and beat him up."

"Listen, Chief Wahoo," said the logger. "Tell this Indian Boy Scout to get back to his tepee and he won't get hurt." The deputy let them both walk off.

Benjamin was okay. He was perfectly okay and he wouldn't talk about it. Not even to Leo.

22

A Vision

GERALDINE SLATER was wearing the ring she found when she began to "see things." That's how she knew the ring was Benjamin's. Because the things she saw were about Benjamin.

The visions began to come at night. Like dreams. Her parents thought they were dreams. Geraldine could read the sign language they used. But once it happened right in broad daylight. When she wasn't asleep at all. When she was wide awake. Then she knew that none of them were dreams at all.

The first time, she saw herself walking along with Benjamin. While she was walking, she opened her mouth and sang an Indian song. The words came perfectly to her lips, even though she had never heard them before. And she sang it to him again and again.

Then she saw someone coming toward them. She was afraid but she kept singing and singing and the figure

came right out of the sea and came closer and closer.
When it was very close, she saw it was a woman. Old.
And sort of horrible. Her brown clothing swirled around
Geraldine's face. And she poured something over Geral-
dine's head.

"You talked in your sleep last night," her mother said
with a little smile.

"Y'mean *sang*," said her brother Harold.

"What was I singing?" She felt a strange odd flutter
at her wrists.

"Mumbo jumbo," he said with a shrug. "Sort of
spooky."

Her mother looked at her a little worriedly. "Did you
have a stomachache?"

Harold said, "Oh, there's nothing wrong with her a
good witch doctor couldn't fix."

Her father laughed. So did her mother. Harold could
be funny sometimes. She guessed they thought he was
funny all the time. It didn't seem so funny to her.

The next time she saw the old lady, the same thing
happened. Only she couldn't stop singing the song. She
wasn't able to stop her mouth from singing it. And Benjamin couldn't either. He took her to an Indian doctor.
And the doctor danced an Indian dance. And a lot of
them made a circle around her and chanted. They rang
bells and shook their hands and their bodies. To get the
song out of her. It wasn't her song. She had got it by
mistake. It was one of theirs.

"Wow!" Harold said when she came to breakfast. "Pop's been yelling at you for an hour. I thought you were never going to wake up."

"You know what?" she said as lightly as she could manage. "That's what I thought too."

The next time Geraldine saw the vision, the brown woman was pulling Benjamin into the water. And Geraldine had to go in herself to pull him back.

"A nightmare," her mother said the next morning. "You had a terrible nightmare."

"It wasn't a nightmare. I wasn't dreaming."

Her father laughed.

"I was there," Geraldine said calmly. "Just the same as I'm here now."

"Eat your breakfast," her mother said sharply, while her face talked like mad in sign language to Geraldine's father. They thought she was spaced out.

When she saw the vision for the last time, Geraldine was walking down the street with Louise Barry.

They were just walking along together and suddenly that song came to her lips and she started singing it at the top of her voice. She tried not to sing it, but it kept flowing out. Like the river flowing into the sea. She wasn't scared. Not as much as Louise was. Louise took hold of her and shook her until the song stopped.

Louise was green-looking. "What did you do that for?"

"I didn't do it on purpose."

"You sounded like an Indian. I couldn't understand a word you were saying. What were you singing?"

"I don't know."

But she did. Because she had been singing that song again. The song that wasn't hers. And she knew what it meant now. She could feel it. She knew it even though she didn't want to.

"Tell me!" Louise commanded.

Geraldine told her. She told her the meaning of the visions she saw. "I think Benjamin Turner is going to die."

Louise laughed. A little shakily. But she laughed. "Honestly, Geraldine, you should go see a psychiatrist."

That night Geraldine took off Benjamin's ring. She gave it to her brother Harold. "I found it," she said. "It belongs to someone in your class." But she didn't say Benjamin. And Harold wasn't the kind to even think to ask.

23

Douglas Digest

Swallows swarming around likely nesting places as warm weather sets in again. Many colds appear after the fine weather last week. Flower plants set out all over town. Boys venture out to peel cascara as funds get low. Only three more weeks of school.

24

Running

For a while Benjamin Turner felt he wanted to die. The town of Douglas was suddenly an ugly place to him.

It was like seeing the underside of a sleek automobile. Leering shafts, pans, batteries, wires, hoses, pipes, tubes, and filters. Layered with dirt and grease. And caked with mud. It was like looking at the hidden part of an iceberg. Under the water was a tremendous hump of sharp edges and startling jagged points.

The streets of the town were rivers ready to drown him. The windows were giant eyes. The people had changed into laughing monsters. Enemies.

He flew around in his car as if he were racing with the thunderbird. He got hauled into the marshal's office and fined three times for speeding. He was like the Indian with a power in him too strong to contain. Running. Behind the wheel of his car he flung himself against the wind. His song was powerless to help him. It was as if he had used it up. Or lost it. For somehow it had slipped away from him. He no longer heard it in his head. He didn't want it anymore anyway. It had proved to be useless to him.

For a while he really didn't care.

He helped Mr. Otis move out to Salt Chuck into a room of an empty summer motel. They used Leo's station wagon to transport Mr. Otis' stuff.

Leo's troller was docked in the boat haven. Its deck was a clutter of winches, reels, sinkers, and other gear. In the center of the deck was a rig with six poles sticking straight up. When Leo was out fishing, the six poles spread out at different angles each holding a fishing line. Each line had about twenty hooks on it. The boat was old and Leo was continually patching and repatching, painting and repainting.

Sometimes Benjamin slept in the little cabin. Leo didn't mind. Sometimes he went over and slept on the floor in Mr. Otis' room. Mr. Otis didn't mind either. They were his friends. Along with Harold. Just about his only friends, he thought.

He didn't pay much attention when he heard the kids at school were going to bust out on a senior sneak. What was happening in Douglas High School seemed like a million miles away. It had nothing to do with him anymore. Or at first he thought it had nothing to do with him.

A senior sneak was against the rules at Douglas High School. Everybody knew it. Though it used to be a big thing in Douglas before the school board outlawed it. There had been no senior sneak in Douglas High School for twelve years.

But there was going to be one this year.

"It's a protest," Harold told him.

Benjamin really wasn't much interested.

"Against the truancy rules," said Harold. "They're old-fashioned. Out of date. We decided we got to protest the present school administration's way of doing things. Some of us kids have been planning it since the night you got kicked out."

"Where you going?"

"What difference does that make? We're just going. Out to the beach I guess. We're not going to school on June one. We're not even going to show up for attendance. We're just going to meet outside. In the parking lot. Like you did. Then we'll take off and not come back until the end of the day."

"Well, have a good time," Benjamin said.

Harold grinned. He looked like a gargoyle. His eyes were all puckered up with the creases of his enjoyment. His hair swirled about his face like frosting on a cake. Benjamin hadn't noticed before. Harold had stopped cutting his hair.

"They'll have to suspend us," said Harold. He sounded terribly happy. He sounded goofy too.

"You're crazy. They're not going to suspend the whole graduating class. No matter what you do."

"Maybe not. But they'll have to do something — won't they? — so they'll change the rules!"

It was not anything that Benjamin could get very excited about.

"Hey man! You know what?" Harold said one day. "We got ourselves three Indian cheerleaders. How's that? From Salt Chuck. The kids voted on it. The Indians won hands down." He grinned as if he had just won the first major battle of the American Revolution. A Bunker Hill. He acted as if there were no discrimination anymore. Like all the problems were taken care of.

"The rest is up to the parents," Harold said. With an owlish expression. "We're getting them primed. For the senior sneak."

"The only good Indian is a dead Indian. Ever hear of that?"

"A hundred years ago."

"The methods have changed. But it's still the same old policy."

Harold shrugged. Amiably. Harold didn't like to argue. You tossed him a ball and he dropped it like a lead balloon.

The School Board asked Benjamin to come to another

meeting. They said they had decided to allow him to be readmitted to Douglas High School on September 7, 1971. Provided he sign something. It was a contract. It listed all the rules he would have to promise not to break. Including throwing snowballs at the windows. That made him laugh. They told him again that he had broken the rules and the reason he had been expelled was because of that and not because he was an Indian. That was a laugh too. They said the contract was for his own good, and asked his father to make him sign it.

His father stood up and said, "I have never forced my son Benjamin to do anything in his whole life."

That surprised the board members. They didn't understand it.

Benjamin did. He had just never thought about it. He couldn't remember his father ever "making" him do anything. Not even for Benjamin's own good. His father never interfered.

In an Indian village, the young children never interfere with the older people either. They don't bother them. It was funny because Benjamin couldn't remember that anybody said anything to them about it. They just didn't do it.

Maybe it was one of the things that had come through hundreds of years of tribe living. No one in Salt Chuck ever interfered with anyone else. Not if he could help it. If he did, the punishment was pretty strong. To an Indian. Sometimes everyone in the village would turn their backs on him. They'd act as if he weren't there. Like a banishment. A purgatory.

Benjamin didn't sign the contract. He didn't care about coming back to school anymore. It wasn't important to him. He learned he could pick up any missing credits from high school at a junior college. And he decided he might do that. But he didn't even know for sure. There were other ways he could get an education. He wasn't sure about anything.

One night he pounded on Louise's door and asked her to run off with him. They could get married. She said she'd think about it.

He thought about it too. And changed his mind.

He discovered that smoking a little grass made him feel good. Made him want to talk. He'd sit in Leo's kitchen, listening a little to the hi-fi. And talking a lot. About himself some. But mostly about what he saw that had to be done to help the kids from Salt Chuck. The whole problem seemed so clear to him. And what was needed to solve it. He was reading a lot. About Indians. The ones in his own tribe. The way they had been. And the way they were. And what was happening to them. Some things goods. But more bad. Too much bad.

"Before the white man came," he told Leo, "nature gave us Indians everything. Even sandpaper that is better than the store kind. Dried dogfish skin. Coarse from the belly and fine from the back."

Leo listened.

"Nature gave the Indian courage, too. You've got to be pretty brave to go out looking for whales in a dugout canoe!"

"There are all kinds of courage," Leo said.

But Benjamin wasn't really listening to Leo. He was trying to hear himself.

He went off for a week. He went over to the city by himself and strode up and down the hills. He did a lot of things. He did things like crazy.

He began to spin like a propeller on a two-engined plane. He was pulled in twice on charge of being a minor in possession of alcohol. He got fined for negligent driving — and for speeding. He was warned. Several times. But he kept on spinning. He whirled from the village to town to city and back again. He was like an unguided missile. A rocket. A satellite plummeted out of orbit. Looking for earth.

He landed. After speeding along the Salt Chuck road and crashing into a fence, he landed in jail. He was relieved of his license. And what they called his freedom. For ten days.

25

Senior Sneak

June 1, 1971

Mr. Haley asked the board what action to take since 52 seniors were absent today from school of a class of 58. Motion was passed that all seniors without acceptable excuses would have their diplomas held back graduation night and they would be required to attend an additional day of school.

June 3

Mr. Haley has received 42 excuses signed by parents of students who were absent on June 1 that the students were ill.

Motion was passed to postpone graduation one day to June 9, 1971.

26

Hero's Journey

BACCALAUREATE June 6, 8:00 P.M.

Processional	Mrs. Lee Juning
Invocation	The Reverend Alexander Peech Lutheran Church
Scripture Reading	Proverbs 1: Verses 2–25 The Reverend Walter Bottinger Douglas Bible Church
Address	THE HERO'S JOURNEY The Reverend Floyd McDougall Douglas Congregational Church
Benediction	The Reverend Joshua Allister Assembly of God Church
Recessional	Mrs. Lee Juning

COMMENCEMENT June 9, 8:00 P.M.

"Pomp and Circumstance" — Sir Edward Elgar
                              Douglas High School Band

Invocation	The Reverend Morris Loster First Baptist Church
Flag Salute	Steven Jeffrey Class President
Presentation of Student Speakers	Mr. Richard Stevenson Superintendent Douglas School District
Student Speakers	Linda Pole Frieda Montgomery Ruth Little Gerald Greg
Student Awards	
Presentation of Class	Mr. Gregory E. Haley Principal
Presentation of Diplomas	Mr. Arthur Bentley Chairman, Board of Directors Douglas School District

"Pomp and Circumstance" — Sir Edward Elgar
                              Douglas High School Band

27

Ebb Tide

"It's rather hard for me to explain what part of life I have just gone through. It's been difficult for my parents and me. Many times I wanted to give up on everything. The thing that kept us all going was my cause. My cause was something which every human being strives for. An identity.

"An identity is something which makes the human being alive. Without it, there is no need to live.

"Right now I'm more confused than anything else. Maybe there is no solution for any of our problems. Perhaps there is . . ."

28

On the Beach

I've BEEN THINKING," said Benjamin.

Harold blew up the fire they had built on the beach. The white tips of the waves caught the moonlight. Shining.

"I never did any real thinking. Not until my brother David died. That's what started me, I guess. I did a lot of thinking sitting in jail."

"That's one of the convenient things about thinking. You can do it any place," said Harold.

Benjamin made a cushion of his sleeping bag for his back. He wasn't a bit sleepy. He leaned against the log. "Confusion. That's the issue — the confusion in our lives. For Indians. To get along in this white world the white man tells us Indians that we must be white men. That we can't be what we were born to be. And this causes confusion. In our minds. In our lives."

Harold's cheeks puffed out. Like a blowfish. His nose turned thin and pointy. The flames spurted up and finally flared again.

"I look at the kids at Salt Chuck. They are not Indians. And they are not white. So they're lost. They don't really know who they are. Or where they belong."

Harold stuck his feet into his sleeping bag.

"We'd like to be proud we are Indians. But the schools don't let us. They ignore the Indian history and the Indian culture. That makes for more confusion because it makes Indian kids ashamed they are Indians." Benjamin crossed his legs. He folded his arms across his chest. And stared over the fire onto the sea.

"You look like a wooden Indian," said Harold.

"Right on." Benjamin's voice crackled. Dry as the old cedar bark used to start the fire. "That's exactly what we are. Wooden Indians. We don't have our culture, our religion, or our identity."

"Ah, come off it, Benjamin. That all happened when the moon was green cheese. You're you. Today. Now."

"Funny. I never really knew who I was. After asking myself for the longest time, 'Who am I?' I finally resolved, 'Benjamin, you've got red skin; you're an Indian.' The thing is — when you know who you are you know exactly what you have to do. You can function."

"Well, I know who I am," said Harold. "But I'm darned if I know what I'm going to do. My mother spends most of her time telling me. And I still don't know."

It was like talking to a telephone pole, thought Benjamin. "Man, you're a stupid ass," he said.

Harold looked up, incredulous with surprise. "Who do you think you're calling a stupid ass?"

"Nobody," said Benjamin bitterly.

Harold chuckled. "You know how to slice it on both sides."

"Sometimes you don't make any sense."

"Well, what's sense?"

Benjamin stretched his legs out and considered the question. "Being yourself. That's sense."

"Maybe what's sense to one person isn't to another," Harold said.

Benjamin stared into the fire.

"Like the senior sneak," said Harold. "You wouldn't believe it. You just wouldn't believe it. They thought holding diplomas off for one day was a *punishment*. They really did."

The firelight reached up into the night in front of them. Logs spat, and fell. Waves sounded.

"They didn't even talk about it being a protest. They thought we were trying to revive an old tradition." Benjamin couldn't tell whether Harold was laughing or gargling. "Anyway, you're out of jail," Harold said. As if it had some connection. He stared at the fire too.

"Man, you know what I'm going to do. If it's the last

thing I do. I'm going to walk me through Salt Chuck the way Indians did before they had to wear white man's clothes."

"Sounds chilly to me."

"Listen. I got an idea for this summer. What I'm going to do is form a junior tribal council in Salt Chuck. That'll help build up pride among kids. About being an Indian. To help erase the feeling of oppression."

"Sounds great." Harold yawned.

"I've got to do it. I thought it all through. I hope it doesn't fail this time. It would beat the Indians down that much more."

"Good idea." Harold yawned again.

"I don't know what I will do this summer if it doesn't work."

Harold said suddenly, "You know, sometimes I can't figure you out."

"I'm an Indian."

"Yeah. Well, explain it to me."

It was too difficult to explain, thought Benjamin. Every Indian knows in his bones that some things have to be kept hidden away inside of you. Carried like a knife blade in a sheath. Safely out of sight. Because if you let it out, it could maybe rip you apart. Maybe that's what beer did to him, Benjamin thought. To all the Indians. Maybe the drinking unzipped the pouch of hidden-away griefs. Let them all fly out. That's the way his brother David acted when he got himself a bottle. A few drinks and he became a wild Indian.

Benjamin laughed. But it was not the kind of joke you could share with a hoquat.

"As I said," Harold said. "Sometimes I can't figure you out."

"You're a white man," Benjamin said.

Harold's voice came out of the hollow of the dark. "What kind of an explanation is that?"

Benjamin kicked at the burning driftwood log stuck in the fire and watched it break apart in the middle. Where the fire had burned through. "As I said, it means I'm an Indian."

Harold crouched before the warm blaze, hugging his knees. The firelight flared up and gave his face a grim white expression. "I still don't see what that adds up to."

Benjamin said slowly, "It means that's the reason everything bad happened."

"It means you've got to see it your way. Or no way. That's what it means," said Harold.

"Well, how do you see it?"

"You really asking me?"

"I really want to know," said Benjamin.

Harold stood up. He stood there stretching the kinks out of the back of his knees. They'd been sitting there most of the night. Benjamin hadn't wanted to sleep inside, that night. Not under any roof. Not after having been in jail for ten days.

Harold stared out past the rolling gray water. Then he dropped down again suddenly. Squatting like an old Indian woman picking grasses for her baskets.

"You went about it wrong," Harold said earnestly. "You went about the whole business wrong. The Indian Culture Club. And getting mad at Mr. Haley. And taking the kids to the dig. And listening to that crazy Mr. Otis. So what happened? He got fired. And you got expelled!" Harold webbed his fingers together and used it like a brush to sweep his hair back off his brow. "Man, you went about it all wrong!"

Benjamin flicked a handful of sand into the fire. He didn't care about being expelled. He could finish his credits at junior college.

"You got the principal mad at you. And you got the whole damn school board mad at you. And you got the town mad at you. And what happened? You landed in jail. That's what happened."

"Had nothing to do with it."

"Sure it did. What did you get thrown in jail for? Speeding. That's what."

"And crashing into a fence in Salt Chuck."

"Well, who cares what happens to an old fence in a stinking little village like Salt Chuck. The marshal sure didn't. He's never paid much attention to what happens in Salt Chuck before, has he?"

Benjamin looked down at his hand. Shoved, knuckle-deep, into the sand. "Why should he? It's on the reservation." He made his hand stay there.

"Right!" Harold jabbed at him with a stiff forefinger. "Your reservation. Who cares?" he said scornfully.

"So what does that prove?"

"It proves you went about it all wrong. As I said. Right from the first."

Benjamin shook his head. "It proves only what I said before. I'm an Indian. And you're a white."

Harold got up. He looked disgusted. He moved around the fire. Kicking at it. "You feel like going for a walk?"

Benjamin didn't answer.

"Well, I feel like taking a walk." Harold went. Heading up the beach. Clumping down into the sand with each step. Like an astronaut walking on the moon.

Before he came back, Benjamin arose. He picked up his stuff. And walked off.

29

Echoes

I hear distant drums,
my ears deceive me.
I see tepees and smoke
drifting from the warm fires.
My eyes play tricks.
I smell cooking meat, pounded
berries and fresh buckskin,
My nose is only teasing.
I feel long braids hanging from
my head.

My hands reach to stroke,
I wake up with tears in my eyes,
I am only dreaming.
The food is eaten,
The fires are cold,
The drums have ceased,
The songs have ended,
The dance is over,
The dancers are gone.
My people, where are they?

30

I Wanna Be an Indian

BENJAMIN walked free down the middle of the street toward the boat haven. The cool morning air tickled his naked skin. Going clear through him as if he were made of woven grasses. Like an Indian basket.

He had left his clothes, neatly folded on the grocery step. It had been a whim to take them off. A desire that he did not know he had. Until he had expressed it. He did it. Because it seemed somehow like the right thing to do. He didn't expect anybody would interfere. Not in Salt Chuck.

He didn't notice the man looking sleepily out of the window at a charter boat office. Or the Indian girl with curlers in her hair at her window across from it. Standing there with her mouth gaping.

Benjamin walked unhurriedly, easily, along the village street. His song came back into his head suddenly. Like day comes back to the land after the night. He sang it to himself. "I wanna be an Indian. I wanna be red. I wanna be free. Or — " He turned down toward the boat haven.

He had asked himself "Who am I?" But it was not enough. He had answered, "I am an Indian." That was not enough. It was not enough to see the problems Indians have either. Or to want to solve them. He had tried. And failed. Maybe because he wasn't important enough. Or strong enough. It was something he hadn't been able to do alone. He didn't have enough power.

Perhaps he needed a special kind of power, thought Benjamin. He looked at the boat-haven water rippling before him. Beyond the mouth of the river, the ocean shouted to him.

He remembered the old bus driver telling the kids how his father had acquired a warrior spirit. It was necessary to dive into deep water, he said. David had tried to get a warrior spirit once himself. He had gone down to the river and dived in a lot of times. Staying under as long as he could. A whirlpool, if you could find one, was the best place, he had said. For it would suck you down.

He had tried weighting himself with a stone. He spit on the stone first until it was covered with saliva. That's the way it was supposed to work. He dove into the ocean from the big rock with the stone to carry himself down. When he awoke he found himself lying on the beach. But he had met no spirit.

David had tried making a raft and fastened himself to it by a long rope. He dived with his spit-covered stone. Leaving it on the bottom, he pulled himself up by the rope. He didn't find the spirit, though. Pretty soon he knew he would never find a spirit. He had never even seen a vision.

Once Benjamin had dreamed he saw a white man carrying an arrow in one hand and a white bone in the other. His brother said that was the same as seeing a vision. In the dream, the white man gave Benjamin a gift. David had told Benjamin what the gift was. It was that all white men would like him.

Benjamin raised his arms and waved them around in the air, laughing. The idea made him laugh some more.

He didn't need the gift of the dream, he decided. What he needed was a warrior spirit.

If he had a warrior spirit, he'd have the power to do all he wanted to do. If he had a warrior spirit, what would it matter if white men liked him or not? What would it matter?

Author's Note

NOT MUCH is known of what occurred in the early morning of June 17, 1971, between the time this Indian youth left the beach and a few hours later when he was found drowned in the waters of the boat haven. The clothes he had last worn were left, neatly folded, on a porch one quarter mile away. In a pocket, on the back of a yellow flyer for an Indian law day program, was his four-line poem, "I wanna be an Indian."

The action of the last chapter is as the author imagined it might have happened.

The youth who was the Benjamin Turner of the story was buried close to his brother in the little graveyard on top of the hill behind the Indian village where he was born.

Special Acknowledgments

I DEEPLY APPRECIATE the help of those who were closely in-volved in the events which this book fictionally relates. I thank them for their cooperation. My thanks as well to the people of the town called Douglas in this story, and to the people of the village here named Salt Chuck who will never completely forget the young warrior who grew up among them. I thank them for so willingly sharing their feelings, thoughts and views with me.

My acknowledgments also to the sources helpful in pro-viding me with pertinent information, particularly the sur-veys and reports made by the state's Human Rights Com-mission, and the news accounts, editorials and Letters-to-the-Editor columns in the newspapers of the area.

The lines of verse quoted in Chapter 29 were written by Pamela J. Morganroth printed in a local newspaper's Letter-to-the-Editor column. The personal statement in Chapter 27 was written by the Indian youth whose life came to an end in the river on June 17, 1971.